P9-CMN-681

Praise for *The Old Success*

"In her books featuring Scotland Yard Superintendent Richard Jury—the most recent of which is *The Old Success*—author Martha Grimes has created a type of mystery all her own. The stories have a cozy structure—but with windows into darker worlds."   —*Wall Street Journal*

"There are many wonderful lagniappes to enjoy, including Melrose's menagerie: a goat named Aghast, a dog named Aggro and a horse named Aggrieved, who gives the lie to his name by running a brilliant if unconventional race."   —Marilyn Stasio, *New York Times Book Review*

"The twenty-fifth Richard Jury mystery continues the Grimes tradition of mixing solid procedural details with deft characterization and offbeat wit."   —*Booklist* (starred review)

"In terms of verbiage, slang and speech pattern, [Grimes] channels the British vernacular flawlessly. Some interesting subplots (one with a race horse, one with a race car and one with an updated take on the Baker Street Irregulars) help to tie up some loose ends and keep the reader guessing as they wait for the surprising big reveal."   —*BookPage*

"In any Richard Jury mystery, the reader can always count on the very witty and amusing banter that is a trademark of the series. But what makes this entry stand out from the usual, aside from the complexity, is the investigative pairing of Jury with Sir Thomas Brownell."   —*Mystery Scene*

THE OLD
SUCCESS

MARTHA GRIMES

THE OLD SUCCESS

A RICHARD JURY MYSTERY

Grove Press
New York

Copyright © 2019 by Martha Grimes

All rights reserved. No part of this book may be reproduced in any form or by any electronic or mechanical means, including information storage and retrieval systems, without permission in writing from the publisher, except by a reviewer, who may quote brief passages in a review. Scanning, uploading, and electronic distribution of this book or the facilitation of such without the permission of the publisher is prohibited. Please purchase only authorized electronic editions, and do not participate in or encourage electronic piracy of copyrighted materials. Your support of the author's rights is appreciated. Any member of educational institutions wishing to photocopy part or all of the work for classroom use, or anthology, should send inquiries to Grove Atlantic, 154 West 14th Street, New York, NY 10011 or permissions@groveatlantic.com.

Published simultaneously in Canada
Printed in the United States of America

This book was set in 12.5-point Garamond Premier Pro
by Alpha Design & Composition

First Grove Atlantic hardcover edition: November 2019
First Grove Atlantic paperback edition: October 2020

Library of Congress Cataloging-in-Publication data is available for this title.

ISBN 978-0-8021-4899-5
eISBN 978-0-8021-4741-7

Grove Press
an imprint of Grove Atlantic
154 West 14th Street
New York, NY 10011

Distributed by Publishers Group West

groveatlantic.com

20 21 22 23   10 9 8 7 6 5 4 3 2 1

To my great and gracious daughter-in-law,
Travis Holland

If I shouldn't be alive
When the robins come,
Give the one in red cravat
A memorial crumb.

If I couldn't thank you,
Being just asleep
You will know I'm trying
With my granite lip.

—Emily Dickinson

PART I
Hell Bay

1

Brian Macalvie looked down at the body of the woman whose face, beneath the lattice of seaweed and wet hair, was oddly serene.

The bay was not. The others who stood with him were soaked, or would have been had the island police not known to wear full-scale rain gear. Macalvie had brought nothing with him from the mainland of Cornwall except Gilly Thwaite, his scene-of-crime officer, and Detective Sergeant Cody Platt. Gilly stood there shivering despite the cape one of the Scilly policemen had settled around her shoulders. Shivering and cursing under her breath at her superior for being one of those who likes to take his time.

It had taken Macalvie and his team less than an hour from the time he'd dropped the phone back into its cradle in Exeter to the moment the light plane landed on St. Mary's, one of the Isles of Scilly, twenty-six miles from Land's End. There was no airport on Bryher, the smallest of the populated islands, so from St. Mary's they had taken the short boat ride with Detective Chief Inspector Whitten.

All in all, Gilly was thinking, a fairly good clip. It was not that Macalvie couldn't move quickly—he could move like lightning—it was that when it came to viewing the dead, he took his time. God, but did he ever take his time. He might as well have been frozen in it, and here was a good place for being frozen. His request to DCI Whitten (the one who'd rung him up) was that nothing be moved, nothing be messed with.

I'll tell the sea, Commander, not to move anything.

Brian Macalvie had been looking at the body for fifteen minutes.

"There are just too many variables, guv," said Gilly. The "guv" was anything but obsequious. It was bad-tempered is what it was.

He had finally kneeled down to study the face more closely, but without brushing aside the dead woman's seaweed-laden hair.

"I mean," Gilly went fearlessly on, "your crime scene has been compromised again and again by the waves and wind." As if to underscore this point, a wave crashed against the outcropping of rocky promontory. Then another. It was like thunder breaking at their feet.

Macalvie looked at her over his shoulder and she shut up.

The island police had already taken photos. Gilly knew her boss hated even the camera's poking about over the scene, as if its seemingly random flashes were witchy, pulling from the dark things which would have been better left there. It was as if the camera were leaching soul from substance, as in the old superstition that a picture captured the spirit and held it.

At his side, DCI Whitten said, "Perhaps whoever did this did it and left—went back to the mainland. Maybe he shared the belief of those ancient people who buried their enemies on islands because that way they couldn't come back and make trouble.

"The irony," Whitten went on to say, "would not be lost on anyone who knew the Isles of Scilly are proof against any disturbance, possibly the safest land in Britain." He looked down at the woman who had been lying there now for two hours, lying still except for the water's lapping at her side, very still and very beautiful, as if she had now become part of the granite of the islands that were declared an area of outstanding natural beauty. "Also designated as a Heritage Coast. Nothing cheap or tawdry." Whitten spread his arms. "Do you see a Starbucks?"

Macalvie snickered. "Not yet."

Gilly had not realized how much tension had built up until the laughter broke it. It was more than the death and the pale body. It didn't stem from a turf war, a jealous guarding of his authority by DCI Whitten. What she saw was quite the opposite: relief. There was relief that this unprecedented crime should be turned over to the Devon-Cornwall constabulary—to Divisional Commander Macalvie.

The mood was not helped by the ceaseless, thunderous crash of sea against rock. This little part of the coastline offered no protection from wind and water. Either the shape of the bay or the promontory seemed to make it worse, as if the rocks out there were a bulwark against the waves, which consequently built up into an even stronger force. It was like a fist beating and beating against a door.

Macalvie, done with staring and breathing in this round of death, got up and motioned for Gilly to go ahead. She veritably fell on the body, as eagerly (she hated to think) as a necrophiliac.

Macalvie looked up the coast and saw lights twinkling. "That the hotel?"

"The Hell Bay, yes."

DCI Whitten had filled Macalvie in as best he could on the brief boat trip from St. Mary's. The Hell Bay Hotel was the only accommodation on Bryher.

They walked over wet sand. "It gets enough custom to stay open?" said Macalvie.

"Indeed, yes. It's considered one of the best small hotels in England, actually."

"Jesus. People are so fond of isolation?" To Macalvie, isolation was a pub shutting down when he was the last one in it.

"Well, yes. I can see its attraction for anyone who has to drive the M2 into London during rush hour. Remember, too, you haven't seen any of this in daylight, in sunshine. It's quite beautiful. This sand is white."

Even in the darkness, it looked ghostly, ghost-sand.

Whitten went on. "I showed our police photo round the hotel, but none of the staff recognized her. I thought I should get right on that without waiting."

"You should. Guests this time of year?"

"A few. Four, I believe she said."

"The owner? The manager?"

"The owners are gone for a bit. Holiday in the Virgin Islands. They left a Mrs. Gray in charge. Quite capable, she seems to be. Didn't go bonkers at the news of a body on her doorstep, practically."

"Any joy there? I mean amongst the guests?"

Whitten shook his head. "No one recognized her. Of course, with all that stuff webbing her face . . . ? Anyway, it's impossible at this inning to know who's telling the truth, who isn't."

Inning. Macalvie liked that. "Is it your coroner's theory that the body had drifted there from somewhere else? One of the other islands, say?" Macalvie had stopped to run his finger round inside his shoe to get out some of the sand.

"Oh, no. Listen: you can do much better on this sand if you just take your shoes off. That's what I do. I mean, when nobody's around."

They both looked a little furtively at the hotel ahead and the small band of police behind. Between, the little stretch of beach glimmered in the moonlight like crushed pearl.

"More fun, too," said Macalvie, taking his socks off also.

Whitten shoved his socks into his shoes, tied the laces together, and hung the lot over his shoulder.

They continued up the strand, the sand a balm to Macalvie's tired feet. "You're right; it is nice. I'd forgotten what it felt like—" Then he realized he'd forgotten because he'd tried to forget those long-gone summers with Maggs and Cassie. Twenty years and it still had the power to stall his feet, to nail him to the spot.

Whitten stopped too. "Commander Macalvie? Are you all right?"

"What? Yeah. Yes. I'm okay." They walked on. It was the mention of the little girl who appeared to have found the body that had started it, he knew. Knowing he was going to have to talk to a little girl. He was not good with children. He seemed only to be able to do it if he got belligerent. There had been that child on Dartmoor, Jessica. He still remembered her, and the memory actually made him smile.

Then the memories swam back again: himself, Cassie, Maggs. Maggie. She had been so beautiful. Where was she now? Was there anywhere in the world you could go once your child has been murdered?

He shook his head, as if to get the sand out of that, too, and said, "You said the body couldn't have drifted into this bay from somewhere else."

"I'm pretty sure not. Well, you see Hell Bay. The force of the waves and wind—I don't see how a body could have gotten *in*. Even the waves pile up there along the promontory."

"Yes, I saw that."

"Which means that she was killed here."

In the dark, Macalvie smiled. He had worked that out. He looked ahead at the lighted panes of the hotel, grown larger now, the building more defined. "So what about comings and goings? The only way to the islands—to any of them—is the way I came, the last part by boat, right? No heliport, for instance?"

"On St. Mary's there's one that's the most used. Then there's one on Tresco. In any event, you'd have to take the launch to get from either of those places to Bryher."

"In the last, say, thirty-six hours, has anyone used the launch?"

"No one. No one's left."

"Then we're looking for either a very strong swimmer—though God knows how one could swim through those waters . . . Is it possible?"

"Possible? Anything's possible, but I've never heard of anyone doing it."

"Or," said Macalvie, watching the windows, behind which he could make out curtains and behind the curtains, moving figures, "the killer dropped from the sky."

"Or," added Whitten, "is still here."

"I was getting to that."

2

"You said it was a kid who found the body."

"Two kids, actually: Zoe Noyes is the older one. Lives with her sister—I guess Zillah's her sister—and their aunt, well, great-aunt to be precise. Cottage is over there." Whitten nodded toward someplace in the distance, east of the bay.

"Then I guess we should start there," said Macalvie.

Whitten walked over to say something to one of his men, as Macalvie told Gilly Thwaite where he was going.

"I suppose she was pretty scared, was she?" Macalvie said as they set off.

"The impression I get is there can never be enough dead bodies for Zoe."

"Swell," said Macalvie, thinking maybe he wouldn't have to do all of the hide-and-seek and cajoling it usually took to get the girl to come out from behind her aunt's skirts.

* * *

Far from having to be cajoled out of hiding, Zoe was all over the house, dragging another chair into the front room where Whitten and Macalvie stood, as if one of them might bolt if there wasn't a chair. Then she ran to get a footstool from its position by the fire.

On the hearth lay a big gray cat, bunched up, paws curled in under its chest. At first Macalvie thought it was sleeping, then decided it was spying, since he could see golden slits just beneath the lids.

Hilda Noyes, the aunt, told Zoe to stop fussing and to sit down if she must. It would clearly have been useless to tell Zoe to leave the room—to go to her own room or anywhere out of sight and sound of the police. Zoe knew a murder when she saw one, or its aftermath, and knew also that she was the star attraction.

Another child, a little girl who looked several years younger than fourteen-year-old Zoe, was introduced as Zillah. That is, was pointed out, for Zillah, unlike Zoe, had no intention of joining the group. Zillah was sitting on the staircase and, upon hearing her name, inched herself farther back against the shadowed wall.

Macalvie could barely make her out, sealed in shadow as she was. He could see clearly only her hair, fine and light as puffball filaments.

Following the direction of his gaze, Zoe said, "That's Zillah, but she won't help."

Her aunt, unhappy with this version of things, said, "Zillah's too frightened to talk, Zoe, as you perfectly well know. Don't make it sound as if the poor child is being stubborn."

"She *won't* talk, Aunt Hilda. She just won't. You can see it in her eyes."

Hilda flapped her hand, brushing her niece's comments away. "Anyway, about this murder, it was Zoe and Zillah that found her—"

Zoe's eyes widened in shock, not at the memory of the corpse but at her aunt's stealing her thunder. "I can tell it!"

Hilda seemed about to protest when DCI Whitten jumped in. "She can, you know, and best she does. I'd like Commander Macalvie to hear it firsthand."

Pleased, but giving Macalvie the once-over as if debating whether or not he was firsthand material, Zoe asked, "What's a commander in the police?"

Whitten answered, "Very high up. Much higher up than me. He works in Exeter."

Tongue literally in cheek, Zoe studied Macalvie. "Are you? Is that right?"

"What? That I work in Exeter?"

"No-o. That you're really high up."

"Not as high as you'd like me to be. Not the commissioner. But let's hear it anyway."

It hardly took persuading. "Okay." Zoe's gaze trailed off and over to a window, black-paned now in the darkness. "I was outside playing with Zillah and then we decided to go over to Hell Bay—"

"Which," said her aunt, "you are not supposed to do, you know that."

Zoe barely stopped in her stream of description and lowered her voice. "We went down to the water's edge. We were collecting shells like we always do and it was dusk—you know, dusk."

(Here was a word she apparently liked for its dark implications.)

"And the waves were really crashing on the rocks. And then I saw this . . . thing. Not up close yet, and I thought maybe it was a seal or something because the thing was so pale. Closer, paler still, like a ghost."

There was a movement on the stair and Macalvie looked towards it. Was Zillah shaking her head in mute protest?

"And I grabbed Zillah's hand and said we'd got to run to the hotel and tell them."

"Where you should have run is straight home."

Zoe didn't bother to comment here. "We told the woman there, the one in charge."

"Emily Gray," put in her aunt. "Emily's a sensible woman; it's good she was there."

"She gave us cocoa," said Zoe.

The cocoa apparently ended the discourse. Zoe picked up the cat and sat down, the cat not at all pleased with this maneuver. He didn't claw the air, but merely wrestled himself out of her arms and slid down to resume his position on the hearth.

Macalvie sat forward, arms on knees. "You didn't see anyone else about?"

"Well, if I did I'd've said, wouldn't I?"

"Yes, I expect you would." Macalvie looked over at Zillah, who again scooted away from the bannister dowels to sit back against the wall. "What happened to your sister?"

Again, Hilda Noyes tried to take over. "She won't say anything. They were out this evening going to—"

Macalvie stomped on this. "Let Zoe tell it, please." Witnesses hadn't a clue, had they?

Hilda dropped back in her chair, chastened. "It's just that Zoe likes to add things on so much—"

"I do *not*. I just say."

"Well, sometimes, dear, what you *say* is not the unvarnished truth."

Macalvie said, "I'll take it varnished." He looked again at Zoe.

She was looking pleased as punch, legs crossed, hands hooked round her knee. "It's Zillah's birthday soon and we were walking over to this little shop that sells everything and I was going to let Zillah pick out what she wanted as long as it wasn't more than two pounds forty. It was—nearly dark. I knew night would come soon, but I didn't want to scare Zillah, so I didn't mention it—"

Macalvie bet.

"—the shop is over near Hangman's Island—"

Another succulent name. Macalvie thought he heard a whimper coming from the stairs.

"You're upsetting Zillah," said her aunt.

Tons Zoe cared.

"That's enough," said Hilda. "It's past their bedtime, Mr. Macalvie—"

"Wait," he said, sitting forward in his chair. "Just one more question."

Hilda sighed, but sat back, resigned.

"Doesn't it surprise you that Zillah would just remain silent after seeing, or partly seeing, this body on the beach? Something else happened, didn't it?"

Zoe's eyes widened; her look at Macalvie was apprehensive.

Hilda was on her feet now and mad as a hornet. "Now, you go. Please go because you're just scaring my Zoe to death."

Macalvie got to his feet. "Frankly, Mrs. Noyes, your Zoe was scaring *me*." He tried on a smile, but that didn't placate her. "Anyway, thank you, Zoe."

As he walked to the door, he put his hand on her shoulder. But as he crossed the doorsill, Zoe came after him.

"Wait. Wait a minute."

"Zoe!" her aunt called.

But Zoe pulled the door shut and they were standing outside in the dark. "Don't pay any attention to Zillah. She's all right."

Macalvie thought this a strange injunction. "Why—?"

"Zoe!" Hilda had come outside. "You've got to come in. I'm sure the police can speak to us tomorrow if they have to." She herded Zoe through the door.

When Zoe looked back over her shoulder at Macalvie, he had a good taste of those arctic eyes. They looked, he thought, hunted.

The door closed but he stood there looking at the cottage for a moment.

Zoe with her wild black hair (and possibly wilder imagination); Zillah, shocked into speechlessness.

Just what he needed in this investigation: two little girls.

"We've questioned all of them, boss—staff who're here right now and four guests. No one seemed to know anything about the vic—"

"She has a name, now, Cody," said Macalvie, snappish enough to make Cody Platt look up from his notebook.

"Sorry. Manon Vinet. Strange name. French, the manager said. They all had exchanges with her, but not about her history, that sort of thing. She didn't talk about herself." Cody stopped, looking rueful. "Failing that, they gave me nothing—nada, nil. Nothing."

"Failing that" being one of Cody's favorite phrases. Macalvie chewed a stick of gum Cody had given him and looked at him. "That's it?"

"'Fraid so."

"How many staff?"

"Four on site."

"So out of those four and four guests you got nothing helpful?" Macalvie wasn't really being critical; he simply found it strange that eight versions of the hotel stay of the victim yielded nothing.

"Nothing beyond the fact they all found her quite pleasant. 'Pleasant' was the operative term."

"Cody, there must be variations on that theme."

"I hear you." Cody thumbed up page after page of notes, shrugged again and said, "I've got it all here, boss. But I can go back to them again—?"

Macalvie shook his head. It fascinated him that Cody never took offense, or if he did, he hid it well. "No, not tonight. It's nearly ten-thirty." He knew the notes were not only copious, but accurate. DS Platt might not have eliciting information down to an art, but his transcript of what was said, well, you could take it to the bank. None better. For all of Cody's apparent (and sometimes real) lethargy, he had an uncanny knack for picking out the bullshit in witnesses' statements.

They were seated at one of the tables in the Hell Bay Hotel dining room, looking out on darkness total enough to be oblivion, and listening to water smashing up against rock. Whitten had returned to St. Mary's with what forensic evidence they'd collected that night; his men were still prowling the rim of Hell Bay.

"Where's Gilly?"

Cody looked ceilingward. "Up in the vic's—sorry, up in Manon Vinet's room."

Macalvie sat for another minute staring at the black glass of the window. Then he rose, saying, "OK. Tell them they can go to bed; tell them not to leave the premises. Get in touch with Whitten and tell him we'll need the helicopter."

Macalvie was through the door when Cody called, "We leaving?"

Over his shoulder Macalvie called back, "Let the DC who brought us over know we want to leave in twenty minutes."

Gilly (Gillian, real name, but she hated it) Thwaite was on her knees, back turned to the door so that she didn't see Macalvie come in. She held a small brush in her plastic-gloved hand and was dusting the squat leg of a heavy bureau.

The door was open; Macalvie rapped on the doorjamb. "What've you got? I hope more than Platt. He's got sod all."

Without even turning, she said, "Are you on his back again? He's good; Cody's very good."

"He may be good, but he's still got sod all."

Gilly stood up and peeled off the gloves. "Which is about what I've got so far, too. Trouble is, I don't think there's much to 'get,' at least not here in her room."

"Okay, come on, pack up. We're leaving in fifteen minutes. Time for bed."

"Thanks to whatever powers may be."

"Who're the others?"

As he turned, she said, "God, what conceit."

Macalvie didn't respond. She was always saying that.

*   *   *

Whatever he had said about going to bed, Macalvie had not gone. Instead, he thought again about interviewing the two girls. He was no good with children anymore. Fortunately, he rarely had to deal with a child as a witness. He had grown increasingly poor at handling them since that summer in Scotland. And if time is the great healer, why was it becoming more painful, rather than less, to deal with them? It was owing to no talent of his that Zoe had told her story at such length. He had not even found out why the girls were living with an aunt instead of parents.

Well, it wasn't his case; it was Whitten's. But he had agreed to help and he didn't want simply to drop it back in DCI Whitten's lap.

Maybe he would hand the next round of questioning the girls over to DS Cody Platt.

Or better yet, to Richard Jury. Whom he was supposed to have met an hour ago in the Old Success.

3

Richard Jury thought for a moment as he looked out over the form-less water of the cove, then said to the man with whom he'd been sharing a table, "Brownell. That name sounds familiar."

As his silence suggested Jury was really trying to chase the name down, Tom Brownell said, "Only if you were police."

"I *am* police. Wait a minute. You're not *the* Thomas Brownell, are you? Of the Metropolitan Police? London?"

"London is definitely the location. You really know the Met, don't you?"

"Very funny. You're *Sir* Thomas Brownell?"

"I try to avoid that."

Jury laughed. "May I buy you another whisky, Tom? Your clear-up rate is legendary. A hundred percent."

"No. More like ninety."

Jury laughed. "Where did you go wrong?"

"Get me that drink and I might tell you. So, are you buying because I have a title?"

"Not at all. Because you don't like it. You remind me of a friend. Once titled. Now not."

"Oh? He did something terrible and got stripped of it?" Brownell sounded hopeful.

"Of them. Earl, viscount, baron, et cetera. No, he simply took advantage of the Peerage Act. He gave them back. He didn't like being called 'lord.'"

"Chap after my own heart. I'm profiling him: canny, straightforward, no-nonsense type."

"That's about right."

"Tell me more about this untitled friend of yours."

"Let me get you that drink, first." Jury collected both glasses and headed for the bar, thinking about Tom Brownell's reputation. Perhaps the man had missed solving one or two cases, but he *was* a legend. Retired several years ago; Jury wondered why. He took the refills back to the table.

Tom nodded toward the door to the bar. "This pub seems suddenly full of police," he said, looking at the two approaching their table. "Friends of yours?"

"No."

"Superintendent Jury?" said DCI Whitten. "Commander Macalvie regrets he's not here."

"Hell, he could have just rung me."

Whitten laughed. "He sent me to take you to him."

"That sounds ominous. Why?"

"Bit of trouble on one of the islands. He'd appreciate it if you'd helicopter over to St. Mary's."

"Why would I do that?"

"He'd like your help."

"Get him on the phone."

Whitten pulled out his mobile, punched in a number. In a few moments he held the mobile out for Jury.

Jury said into it, "This was your reason for meeting me, Macalvie?"

"It is now," said Macalvie.

4

Whitten had shown him the police photos of Manon Vinet, and Jury had looked at them for longer than necessary. He was taken with the symmetry of a face that might have been constructed by a master architect.

They crossed the launchpad and got into a police vehicle driven by a constable. "They're still organizing the boat trip to Bryher."

As they pulled away, Jury asked, "Why not the helicopter?"

"Because St. Mary's and Tresco are the only islands where a helicopter can land. To travel between the islands, it takes a boat. One usually leaves around early evening, but not today. Today, we requested that nobody leave."

"How was that request received?"

"By the people who live there, with their unflagging equanimity."

Jury smiled. "There's a message there somewhere. What is it?"

Whitten said, "We live fairly undisturbed lives here. Especially those on Bryher. It's the smallest of the lot and has the smallest population. Seventy-five, somewhere around there. Here we are," he added, as the car pulled up by a ferry.

"Add the number of tourists to that."

"We counted about a dozen. Only four at the Hell Bay, the others visiting residents."

"You could monitor any private craft?"

"Oh, yes. There are very few of those, and remember, this is the Atlantic we're talking about, which is not the main venue for pleasure craft. But I've made a note of those who do maintain private boats; they're in the folder. Those people are in the bulb business." To Jury's inquiring look, Whitten said, "Tulips, narcissi. We do a lot of business in that line. It's the perfect climate. Flowers and tourists, those are our industries here." He added, "A murder won't do a lot to bolster Bryher's tourist trade, will it?" His smile was tight.

Jury said, "That can work both ways. I'd predict you might have a run of tourists. People are extremely curious when it comes to sex and murder. And the *crime passionnel* can sell a lot of tickets."

"What makes you think this is one?"

"Nothing at all except she's a beautiful woman, and beautiful women often ignite murderous feelings—jealousy, rage—in husbands and lovers. Was she here alone?"

As Whitten opened his mouth to reply, a police constable came up to them. "Boat's ready. Let's go."

As the boat lunged along, slapping at the sea, Jury had to agree with Whitten that this wasn't a venue for pleasure boating. And when they approached the northwest corner of the island, Jury decided it wasn't a venue for pleasure, period.

Yet in its own way, and depending on who was looking at it, Hell Bay was beautiful, if you could take nature unchained, untrammeled and with one hell of an undertow. Pitch-black, the steep, high face of the rocks rose on each side of the bay, and the sound of water crashing against them made it hard to speak in a normal tone. They had to raise their voices.

"Scylla and Charybdis," said Jury. "Monsters in the sea in the *Odyssey*. An impossible passage for a ship."

"Sounds about right," said Whitten.

"Body's here," said Macalvie, looking down at the body of Manon Vinet. Sand had now been swept into small hillocks around her. "Of course, the sand has been swept by wind, so it's not the same. But you get the idea."

"'You get the idea' has never made much of a crime scene, Macalvie." Jury knelt down beside the body. "Gunshot. What kind?"

"Service revolver. Something like a Webley, Smith & Wesson. Probably .38. Close range. We haven't found it. No prints either—I mean, the sand."

"'Something like' and 'probably' . . . I get the idea."

"Oh, come on, Jury. We didn't bring the forensic lab with us. And the scene tells you something, doesn't it? Anything would have been washed away by incoming tides. I expect the shooter knew that."

"It must have been some kind of meeting. Two people wouldn't have been strolling along the beach and just happened on one another. Not with a gun in one of their hands. Pretty odd place for a rendezvous, nevertheless. Who called this in?"

"Manager of the Hell Bay Hotel. Just along there."

"So she was the one out for the stroll?"

"Not exactly. It was a couple of kids."

Jury sighed. "Is this your blood-out-of-a-turnip turn, Macalvie? Why don't you just give me the information instead of me having to pry it out of your mouth like a rotten tooth? You asked for my help, remember?"

"You bet. Only this stuff you don't need to know right at the moment. We're on our way back to Land's End and Exeter. On the boat you just—"

"Then why in the bloody hell didn't you just *leave* me on Land's End?"

"I should have thought that obvious, Jury." He actually sounded hurt. "I wanted you to see the crime scene." Macalvie started to turn away. "Oh, and—"

Jury levelled a look at him. "'Oh, and' what?"

"Maybe interview the ones who found her."

5

When Jury got back to Land's End, the bar of the Old Success appeared to be closed or closing.

Yet Tom Brownell was still sitting at the same table, still drinking what looked like the same drink.

"You waited for me?"

Tom nodded. "Knowing Brian, I figured he'd toss you off that island when he was through with you. Me, I looked for a place to eat, since this one is closing down. How about it? There's a crummy little caff just along the street I've been to several times when I'm tired of the Land's End cachet. I'm starving."

"Great. And thanks for waiting."

"So what was the trouble on the island?"

"Woman got shot on the beach at Hell Bay."

"My God, I guess that is trouble. Any details you can give me? Or is this what we call an 'ongoing investigation'?"

"Well, it's not mine, in any event. It's Macalvie's. But it is ongoing—"

"Say no more. Let's eat. Come on. My car's out in the vast car park."

Which held about five cars, of which Tom's Ford Cortina looked to be the oldest.

The "crummy little caff" lived up to its description—cold, Naugahyde booth seats and unpeopled by anyone but a group of up-all-night teenagers playing the jukebox, smoking God only knew what and occasionally taking passes at the snooker table in a small side room.

The single waitress was caff-unhappy, taking their order in surly silence before bringing back tea in thick, chipped mugs.

Tom raised his. "Perfect, right down to the chips. Cheers."

"You were talking about your granddaughter. Do you see her often?"

Tom shook his head. "Not since Daisy died."

"Her mother?"

"Her name was actually Drucilla but she hated it and insisted we call her Daisy. She was in her early forties." Tom paused. "Suicide, according to the medical report."

Jury rocked back in his chair. "My God, Tom. How terrible. But you said 'according to'—which sounds as if—"

"I'm still finding it hard to believe. Though all of the evidence pointed that way."

The waitress chose that moment to put down plates of eggs and sausage that had Tom looking at the food as if he'd never eaten it before. Then he said, "Sydney has grown far more introverted and far less trusting. At least of me. She doesn't really want to talk to me in any real sense." He set down the fork he'd just loaded up with sausage and egg without eating.

"Why is that, Tom?"

"She's disappointed that I couldn't sort out what happened to Daisy."

"That's expecting an awful lot, isn't it?"

"Yes, but that's what grief often does: turns something impossible into something possible. Turns something unpreventable into the preventable. And who knows but what she's right? I was very close to my daughter, after all. Sydney has some idea that I should have known something was wrong, being such a hell of a good detective."

"But your daughter supposedly committed suicide." Jury frowned.

"That's what I should have sorted." Now he put down the piece of toast, untasted. "The thing is, Daisy just wasn't the—" He stopped and shrugged.

"The type? That what you were going to say?"

Tom nodded. "Which we know is absurd. There is no type."

"Not necessarily absurd. There's no 'type.' Anyone could be driven to kill himself given certain circumstances. Of course, some people would be more likely to do it than others." Jury knew he wasn't saying anything at all, just chewing air, and stopped.

One of the kids moved to the jukebox and shoved in a coin.

The quivery nasal of Roy Orbison was replaced by the silky tones of Nat King Cole.

Tom went on. "The thing is, as I said, we were really close. Always had been. And Sydney couldn't seem to understand why I didn't pick up on her mother's obvious distress."

"For one thing, it wouldn't have been obvious."

"Sydney would have thought, maybe not to others, only—" He reached for his pack of Silk Cuts, pulled one out, and looked at it like a man trying to decide whether to quit smoking. "Only I'm Tom Brownell. The great success. The one with the perfect clear-up rate. But I couldn't detect my own daughter's mental anguish. I couldn't see the signs; I couldn't read the evidence."

"Come on, Tom, don't—"

"If you tell me don't be so hard on myself, I might hit you." The match he lit flared weakly, went out.

Nat Cole's voice flared, much like the flame, on "it's in-*credible*—" and died down.

Tom lit another match. That died too.

Jury was about to take out his ancient Zippo, then thought better of it. "I wasn't going to tell you that. I was going to say, don't let forensics outweigh your intuition."

Over the third lit match, Tom said, "No you weren't. Forensics is forensics." The match burnt Tom's fingers before it died. He regarded the cigarette uselessly. He shrugged.

Jury thought this was not a man to shrug off anything. There was a mystery here, a deep and disturbing one. "What was she like? Daisy?"

Tom looked at the cigarette he couldn't light and then tilted his head toward the jukebox as Nat Cole wound down. "That."

"'Unforgettable.'" It wasn't a question.

There wasn't an answer.

6

"I 'm in!" declared Mrs. Withersby, standing with her mop and pail hard by the window-table in the Jack and Hammer, at which sat the pub's regulars and Long Piddleton's most prominent citizens. Withersby, herself the small town's most prominent char, gave not a whit for the vast wealth and fame of the indolent lot sitting at the table.

"But in what category do you picture yourself, Withers?" said Marshall Trueblood. He had just read them the article about family rentals, a new enterprise that Trueblood wished he had thought of himself.

"What in heaven's name could they be thinking?" said Vivian Rivington. "It's ridiculous."

"Just what it says: if you want a family, or any part of one, you can hire one. Husband, wife, kids, cousins. They're all rentables . . . Oh, don't look so horrified, Viv. Just consider the time and effort saved in searching for and finding your own husband, marrying him and then being disappointed. With this new thing you just send him back and get someone else."

"I do see one big problem with that," said Diane Demorney, who could find a big problem with anything, from the ratio of vodka to vermouth to hiring a husband.

"What?" said Joanna Lewes, who could write an entire suite of books without a big problem.

"Alimony," said Diane. "I wouldn't get anything, so what would be the point, anyway?"

Vivian said, "That's not the only reason to have a family."

"I'm not talking about a *family*." If there was one thing Diane Demorney didn't need, it was a family.

"There *is* love, Diane."

About to pull a cigarette from her silver case, Diane just stared.

Melrose Plant, who had turned in his seat to look out of the bay window, saw his aunt stumping along the pavement with Lambert Strether, apparently headed in their direction. "Here comes Agatha. Not a word." He tapped the *Times*. "Keep this amongst us."

"Amongst us," however, included the *London Times*. They were to discover this when Agatha and Strether entered, she with a copy of the paper taken from the doorstep of her neighbor, Mr. Simmons. As they sat down, she pointed out this little business-theory of relativity, saying, "The most absurd thing I've ever come across. It's called 'FamilyHire.' Can you imagine anything worse?"

"Yes," said Diane, "actually having to buy one."

"Oh, I don't know," said Melrose. "Apparently, if you wanted, you could offer yourself for hire. I think it's a rather good idea."

"You're just being argumentative, Melrose."

"No, I'm just being available. Might someone not like to hire an earl? A viscount? Someone to lend one's dinner party a bit of tone? Indeed, I've considered from time to time renting Ardry End. This way I could rent it and everything in it, owner, staff—I could hire out Ruthven, Martha, even Pippin. There are all sorts of possibilities. You could even hire a policeman. I wonder if Richard Jury would be interested. Or, if you wanted to smarten up your drinks party, you could rent an author." He looked at Joanna Lewes. "My God, the possibilities are endless!"

"Well, don't talk about 'renting' people. You don't want to be considered a 'rent boy.' That's what brought down Oscar Wilde."

"Somehow, Diane, I can't imagine anyone making that mistake with me." Melrose's mobile sounded its little chime, an event so rare that he looked all round the room and finally determined it was his own phone. He pulled it out. It was Richard Jury.

"Richard! Where are you?"

"Cornwall. I want you to get out your horse trailer and take Aggrieved to Bedford."

Melrose took the phone from his ear and stared at it. "I beg your pardon?"

"There's a farrier just outside of Bedford named Sydney Cooke. She's got her own business, called 'Horsepitality.' Don't blame me for the name. This might have some connection with a death on Bryher Island—you know, in the Scillies—"

"I don't know what in hell you're talking about, no."

"Come on, don't give me a hard time over this. Just do as I ask. You're the one with the horse."

"How about the Queen? She has a bunch—"

"Very funny. I've just been with Brian Macalvie on Bryher, where a woman was murdered who has some connection with—maybe this will get your interest—your Flora Flood."

"She's not mine, but it does get my interest, yes."

"The victim is a French woman who looked after Gerald Summerston when he was ill."

"Fine. But why don't *you* talk to this horse person?"

"Because she won't talk to a copper. Her granddad is a famous one, Tom Brownell, and she won't talk to him about her mother's death—"

"Hold on, hold on. I'm trying to follow this. So her mother died in suspicious circumstances and you think this—what's her name?"

"Sydney Cooke. I think she knows something and you're very good at prying information out of people. She doesn't like people; she's crazy about horses. So I need a horse person."

"Get Diane to do it. She knows all sorts of arcane things about horses and she's sitting right here."

"You mean like that horse-racing walk-around thing?"

"I don't think 'walk-around' is the right word, but—" The mobile was yanked from his hand by Diane. "Superintendent, you mean '*walk-over*.' It hardly ever happens. Spectacular Bid did it in the Woodward Stakes in—I don't remember the year. '*Walkover*.' A horse that runs by itself because it's so incredible no other horse will take it on. Here." The "here" was for Melrose, to whom she returned the phone.

"As I said, let Diane talk to the girl."

"No," said Diane. "To whatever." She held up her glass toward Dick Scroggs, who was chewing on a toothpick behind the saloon bar.

Strether broke into this phone business, announcing his own welcome by asking, "What are you all drinking?"

They knew it was a hint and not an offer, and each one chimed in with his separate request.

"Can't expect me to remember all that, can you?" Strether fluttered his fingers as if he were about to bring down the house with a piano concerto, but only brought down the handle of Mrs. Witherby's mop on his shoulder.

"Gin. That's easy enough, ain't it?"

Caught, Strether brought out his old wallet, creaked it open, and every moth in town made its weary way home. "Uh, I'm a bit short today. We should really have a Barclay's branch in town."

"In this village?" said Vivian. "Hardly. There's a branch in Sidbury, right next door, so to speak."

"Want me to run you over?" said Trueblood.

"Uh, no, no," said Strether, returning his wallet to a dusty pocket.

Trueblood caught Dick Scroggs's attention and circled a finger round the table for refills.

"Why would you want a bank in Long Piddleton, Mr. Strether?" said Joanna Lewes. "You don't even live here."

"But I soon will do." He smiled a toothy grin.

"You're actually *buying* a place?"

"Not buying. I'm negotiating with the owners of Watermeadows to let that little cottage on their property."

"*What?*" said Melrose, alarmed that Strether would be living next to Miss Flood when he himself had barely got to know her! "Do you mean the Floods? But they don't own Watermeadows."

"No, but they're free to let that carriage house. Lady Summerston gave them the run of the place."

How in hell could Strether know what Lady Summerston did or did not do, for she, the owner of Watermeadows, had been absent for some months and wouldn't have had him as a candidate for cottage rental for all the money in the world, which he clearly didn't have. But Eleanor Summerston had a large part of it. Having turned over Watermeadows temporarily to close friends but distant relations, the Floods, Lady Summerston had returned to her house in Belgravia.

"There you are, Melrose!" said Agatha. "We'll have Lambert for a neighbor!"

Since his aunt wasn't even a neighbor, that was unlikely. "If you call being a quarter of a mile away neighborly, Agatha."

"Don't be so literal," she said as Dick plunked a sherry before her, for which Trueblood and Tio Pepe would remain forever unthanked.

"One has to be," said Melrose, grimly. He decided at that moment that he would visit Watermeadows, something he had never done for he was afraid of seeming intrusive. But this matter needed to be intruded upon.

7

"He just turned up at the front door," said Flora Flood, shrugging. Melrose smiled. "You mean, like I did."

"No, not at all. He came on his horse. And I didn't mean you aren't welcome." She beamed her welcome.

Melrose certainly *had* turned up immediately after leaving the Jack and Hammer. He imagined turning up in a Bentley was a bit more acceptable than turning up on a horse. "It's none of my business, Miss Flood—"

"Oh, Flora, please."

"Flora. As I said, none of my business, but—"

"We'll make it your business. Come on into the library." One of her legs was in a brace and dragged.

He had met up with Flora Flood a few times before, but always in the Blue Parrot, a scruffy pub off the Northampton Road. And from their brief, Blue-Parrot-relationship, he realized he knew absolutely nothing about her, including what had happened to her leg.

"You must find it hard, keeping this place up." Melrose had just stopped himself from asking why she didn't have a butler.

"The thing is, Uncle Frank—who's seldom here anyway—and I don't have staff. And Aunt Eleanor naturally took Crick with her to London. He's sort of her life's blood."

Remembering the condition of Crick, Melrose wondered whether the man could even be his own life's blood. He should be working at Borings. "It's an awfully large place to be managing on your own."

"There's not that much to do. Would you like some tea?"

"I'd love some tea."

"Right. I'll be back in a few minutes."

"Please don't go to any—" But she'd already gone. He'd forgotten she'd be doing it herself.

While she was in the kitchen, Melrose had a look at some pictures hanging on the wall around the fireplace mantel. He recognized Lady Summerston in several of them, but not the group of men around her. A hunting party, it appeared to be, for several of the men were looking self-important with their shotguns on display. Melrose was surprised to see, in one of them, Lady Summerston holding a shotgun. She was the only woman in the party. He studied the surroundings. In the background was a large house, mansion-large. He wondered what connection this estate had to the Summerstons.

When Flora reappeared with a tea tray, Melrose moved quickly to take it from her and set it on a coffee table, which he cleared of a large vase of cut flowers.

"Thanks," she said, picking up the silver teapot.

"I was looking at the pictures there—" He nodded toward the mantel. "Are they of an estate somewhere?"

"Yes. Gerald Summerston's family home. It's quite large. Or was. I don't know what it is now." She held up the sugar bowl, then the jug of milk.

"Both, but not much of either, thanks. Are some of those of a shooting party? And does your aunt shoot?"

"Oh, my goodness, yes. She's a better shot than most of the men; that's probably why they're looking so grim, standing round her." Flora laughed.

"Your uncle stays in London, then?"

She nodded, sipped her tea. "He doesn't care for the country. I do. This place is so wonderful—But go on. Tell me about this Mr. Strether. Is his name really Lambert?"

"'Fraid so."

"Henry James would probably rather face down that audience for his poor play than face Mr. Strether."

"Poor Henry. Though it's hard to think of James as 'poor' in anything. You know, I actually took over Lamb House in Rye for a short while when—" But he didn't want to bring up the death of Billy Maples. That would sidetrack them for the rest of the afternoon.

"When what?"

"The National Trust's resident had to vacate the place early. Lamb House was fascinating. But back to the present Lambert Strether. When I heard him talking about it, I was a little concerned for you because Strether isn't the best candidate for a tenant." Melrose told her about Strether's various schemes without actually saying "con man."

She said it for him. "He's a con artist. Good grief."

"Artistry has little to do with it. But were you actually looking to let your carriage house?"

"Heavens, no. Especially since it's not ours."

"I'm happy to hear that. I'd hate to have the man as my neighbor. He'd be forever at my place. My aunt is his particular friend. And she's forever at my place."

"I don't believe I know her."

"Perhaps you could join us, say, for dinner one evening."

"That would be grand."

Now, though, he wasn't sure how to proceed. His shyness irritated him. "What I'd like to do is get a few friends together." He was thinking of Trueblood and Vivian, and Jury was to come for a visit the following weekend . . . Wait a minute! Would he want to put Richard Jury in the same room with Flora Flood? Was he mad? Richard Jury was the "ideal man" for any woman over fifteen. No, forget fifteen! For any female old enough to talk. "Do you know the owner of the antiques shop on the High Street, Marshall Trueblood?"

"I've spoken with him when I've been in there. He's very entertaining."

"He is indeed. A few of us gather in the Jack and Hammer quite often. Have you been in that pub?"

"Yes, but I don't stay. It's not like the Blue Parrot. I mean, it's quite a nice pub, but in the Blue Parrot you find people by themselves. The Jack and Hammer has groups—"

Groups? Plural? He thought the only group he'd ever seen was his own.

"—and I feel, you know, left out. So I walk to the Blue Parrot. The walk is good for my leg, too."

This description of the pubs, the "left-outness," and the leg struck Melrose as extremely sad. "What happened to your leg? I mean—"

"How did it come about? Auto accident. I was in the passenger seat and the bonnet crumpled when we hit an embankment."

"I *am* sorry." He paused. "Look, you'd be welcome to join us at the Jack and Hammer."

"You wouldn't really like that. I'd change the chemistry." Then, as if she thought that response ungracious, she said, "But dinner, that would be really nice. If it's not too many people."

"I don't know too many people." Melrose got up, set down his cup. "All right. I'll see to rounding up these people. But right now I'd better be off."

"I'm glad you came."

"Next time, I'll come on a horse."

8

The next afternoon, Mr. Blodgett had interrupted his sunning himself in his Florida room to help Melrose load Aggrieved into the horse trailer purchased just that morning in Northampton. Mr. Blodgett, whose mild hermit-temper was much like the horse's, was far better than Momaday—the grumpy groundskeeper and stableman, who seemed to hate stables, grounds and every animal on them. He liked to sling a rifle over his shoulder and take aim at anything that moved.

Melrose feared for the lives of Aggrieved, Aghast and Aggro—especially the dog, for Aggro ran around, whereas the horse and the goat merely hung around rubbing against trees and nibbling grass. Aggro loved to herd Aghast and moved the goat in circles. Aghast had little else to do but join in this game. Melrose considered getting another goat to keep Aghast company and make more of an inroad on "herd."

He wanted to get rid of Momaday and asked Mr. Blodgett if he would consider taking on the role of groundskeeper. "Not that you have actually to 'keep' the grounds. We have gardeners to do that, but to chase off the odd poacher" (whom Melrose had never in his life seen, but who Momaday swore was around in order to justify the rifle). Momaday had seen far too many American Westerns, especially Clint Eastwood's, as he liked to narrow his eyes and blurt out "punk," a word that must have been reserved for rabbits and squirrels, since he had never actually leveled it at Melrose.

Melrose had heard him say it as he raised his rifle and aimed into the trees: "Punk!" *Bam!* Fortunately, no lifeform hit the ground, nothing but a little shower of leaves. Melrose had admonished Momaday time and again for shooting rabbits, to which the groundskeeper had replied, "Well, if you want your lettuces et up, okay."

Lettuces? They were growing lettuce?

So Melrose had offered Mr. Blodgett twice the salary he was getting as a hermit, and Blodgett had said, "But that's paying me too much, m'lord."

"'Too much' is as the payer assesses the necessity of the job, Mr. Blodgett."

That made no sense to Blodgett, but he heartily agreed.

Before he left with Aggrieved, Melrose told Ruthven that Richard Jury would be joining them for dinner and that he, Melrose, would be back around five or six from Bucks.

Melrose, having hauled the trailer to Newport Pagnell, found Horsepitality in a huge barn and followed the sound of metal striking metal to a room at the back.

He had expected someone short and wide, not this slim girl with a clear forehead, mint-green eyes and a perfect nose. And then he recalled that Jury hadn't given a physical description, but had talked about personality and temperament—a female Momaday of sorts: pugnacious, not very friendly and a good shot. That last attribute was not Momaday-ish, as he was terrible.

The rest of Jury's description had failed when she said, "May I help you, sir?" The tone was mild, the expression welcoming, the face beautiful if a little soot-blackened.

"You're Miss Cooke?"

She nodded.

Melrose looked round the place—the fire, the tools, the blowtorch. "You're very young to be doing this kind of work."

She smiled. "One has to start somewhere."

One needn't start at all, he thought. "There's no farrier near where I live and you were highly recommended to me. I hope it's all right that I've brought my horse. I think he needs re-shoeing." Was that a word? he wondered as he inclined his head in the horse trailer's direction.

"Okay, let's have a look." She put down her tools and they went outside. "I'm not really a blacksmith, you know. But I've had enough training that I can shoe a horse."

"That's more training than I've had." Melrose opened the box and Aggrieved turned his head.

"What's his name?"

"Aggrieved."

She laughed. "I like that. Aggrieved." She appeared to be speaking not to Melrose but to the horse. "Come on, Aggrieved." Sydney placed her hand on the horse's rump and he moved toward the open door. Melrose was surprised at the horse's willingness.

"Come on." She patted his rump and Aggrieved moved slowly all the way out.

"My word. How do you do that? We had a real fight to get him in."

"'Fight' might have been the problem. The resistance goes back and forth, just as it does with people. I think it's better, you know, with animals to play it as it lays."

He did not understand the meaning of that negotiation, but it certainly seemed to work for her. "But you do occasionally have the horse that won't respond to that easy treatment?"

As she took hold of Aggrieved's halter (with one finger, he noticed), she shrugged and said, "Once or twice."

"What do you do then?"

"Walk away." As if to demonstrate, she and Aggrieved walked away from Melrose.

This irritated Melrose, as if he himself were the recalcitrant one in the crowd. "I don't see how that would work."

"Are there really any situations you've come up against that you can't walk away from?"

Melrose tried to think of one, couldn't—except for murder. "You must be a horse whisperer."

"No. Maybe Aggrieved is. It's the horse, not the human, that does the whispering. I think that word has long been misunderstood."

They seemed to be so far away from the subject of murder, Melrose had no idea how to bring it up. Then he thought of the Ryders. "I got the horse from Ryder Stud in Cambridge. Do you know it?"

With an arm embracing Aggrieved's front leg, she said, "I don't believe I do."

"They have a tragic history." Melrose told her about the kidnapping of Nell Ryder and the horses kept at that farm.

"How awful." But Melrose's story elicited no personal history from Sydney Cooke.

He said, lamely, "You must have a horse."

"More than one, actually. We have stables."

"On your property, you mean?"

"It's called Heron House. It's my aunt's. Great-aunt's, to be exact."

Melrose feigned astonishment. "But that's a vast estate. I passed it on my way to the village."

"It's been in the family for decades. My great-grandmother passed it to my grandmother, then to my aunt. I'm next in line, I expect."

It seemed to be put as a question, and she looked at Melrose as if he were the estate attorney who had come to discuss her inheritance. "Well, there'd be your mother first."

"She's dead. I don't think Aggrieved needs front shoes. These seem fine." Aggrieved's hoof was returned to the ground and his right rear leg lifted into Sydney's aproned lap.

"Your father, then?"

At first she didn't respond. "You mean Dan Cooke? He wasn't my father. He was . . . Mum's second husband."

"Oh." It sounded as if she wanted to disavow any relation to the man.

In another half an hour, she had set down the horse's rear foot, and now, rose. "Aggrieved, you have nice new shoes."

Aggrieved was stomping his rear hooves.

"You can see he's pleased. I wouldn't be surprised if that old shoe was hurting." She frowned.

"Oh, Lord, I hope not."

"Who looks after him?"

"An idiot."

She laughed. "Well, then—"

"The situation is being corrected."

"Good." Sydney turned and looked about the barn. "Well, you're my last customer, so I'll pack up and go home. We can get Aggrieved into his trailer . . . I wonder, though. Would you like to come and have a look at my horse and stable?"

Melrose was surprised by this invitation. "I would, yes. Very much."

"Come on, then. You can follow my truck. The house is only a mile or so."

Aggrieved went into the horse box as easily as he'd come out of it. Melrose got into the cab as Sydney got into her small truck, and he followed her to the main road.

They drove through a wide expanse of technicolor—green grass along a smooth dirt road at the end of which was a stone house, large but not imposing. Off to the right, on a narrow side road, stood the barn and stables. Melrose pulled up beside Sydney's truck.

"We'll get Aggrieved out, don't you think? We've a ring, right over there." She nodded beyond the stable. "Would you like to ride Aggrieved, Mr. Plant, now he's reshod?"

He had secretly known this would come up in some form. "Uh, no; my leg has been bothering me lately. Actually, the horse threw me the other day."

Not only did Sydney look at him in disbelief, but Aggrieved turned his head and looked, if a horse could, outraged. "No, he couldn't have done . . ."

Afraid perhaps he'd blown his cover, or Aggrieved's, Melrose said, "Well, I admit I kind of did the throwing. We were jumping a low hedge and I—"

"Thought so." Sydney laughed and stroked her pal's neck again. "Would you do me a favor, then?"

"Of course." *As long as it's nothing to do with getting up on a horse.*

"Could *I* ride him?"

"We'd both be delighted."

"Just a tick, I'll get my saddle." She was in and out of the stable with a horse blanket and a handsome, blood-red leather saddle, which she slid over the blanket. In another few moments, she was up and in the saddle.

"You look as if you belonged there. Aggrieved looks intensely pleased."

Sydney laughed. "No he doesn't. He's just putting up with it. Come on."

Melrose walked beside them as she led the horse to the ring. She took him from a trot to a canter and then was off on a gallop that astonished his owner. She rode Aggrieved around the ring twice and then drew him up to where Melrose was standing beside the fence.

"This horse is the wind! He's the fastest I've ever ridden. Of course, I'm not a jockey; I'm not that fast, but . . . haven't you ever raced him?"

"He was retired when I got him from Ryder's. It didn't occur to me . . . "

"How old is he? I'd say four or five, looking at his teeth."

"Isn't that old to be racing?"

"Of course not. And he loves it; I can tell. Don't you have a ring? You really should let him run."

Oh, dear. Was he going to have to shovel out a circle? "That takes a lot of space, doesn't it?"

"Only about a hundred twenty feet, maybe a little more. With good drainage. But you have a lot of land, don't you?"

Did he?

They led Aggrieved back to the Cooke stable and to the horse trailer. Melrose said, "Aggrieved doesn't want to go. He even looks as if he's crying."

"Crying?" She looked concerned and went around to study the horse's face. There was what looked like a tear running down it. "Oh, dear."

"You can see he's sad."

"Nothing to do with sadness. He might have an eye infection. Have you seen this before?"

"No, not at all."

"Well, keep an eye on it, will you? Better to call in a vet, I think, though it may be nothing at all."

"But it might be something. And you're as good as any vet. Look, I wonder if you'd like to come to Ardry End—that's my place—and have dinner tomorrow night?" Melrose was inspired by Aggrieved's possible minor illness.

She was far more surprised. "Me? Dinner?"

"You'd be doing me a great favor, as you could check up on Aggrieved. There are just a few friends coming. I'm no more than fifteen kilometers away. I'd be glad to send a car for you."

"Well . . . "

"Please do. And you can see how Aggrieved is doing."

She smiled. "Thanks. Yes, I can do that. Just tell me the place and time and how to get there. I can drive."

"Around eight o'clock?" He took out his little notebook and jotted down directions. "It's been a pleasure." He tore out the page and handed it to her.

It took her five minutes to get Aggrieved into the trailer, longer than it had taken to get him out. He didn't seem to want to go.

9

"I had no trouble getting Sydney Cooke to talk to me," said Melrose, when they were seated in the library with drinks in their hands.

"You carted Aggrieved along in a trailer?"

"That's what you told me to do. I don't see why you couldn't have talked to her. She's quite accessible."

"You've noticed I don't have a horse," said Jury.

"Well, it's true you're always showing up in one of Scotland Yard's old bangers."

"New Scotland Yard doesn't have stables."

"And did you read up?" said Melrose.

"On what?"

"Horses, of course."

"No. I read up on the case. The death of her mother, as I told you."

"Well, she won't talk to you about it."

"I think maybe she will."

"Why?"

"I know her grandfather. Who else is coming to dinner?"

"Only Diane and Marshall."

"You didn't invite Miss Flood?"

"No. I didn't know how."

"My Lord. You talk like a poor inexperienced teenager."

"That's pretty much what I am, to hear Agatha."

"What's she like?"

"Agatha?"

"Ha ha. Miss Cooke."

"Quite charming. Pretty. Smart. I told her you worked at the Yard. I let her think you were the janitor."

"That's what Racer thinks I am."

Melrose chortled. "Diane is bound to come up with horse arcana; she'll fill her thimble of knowledge to the brim."

The door knocker fell with a thud and would have thudded again had Ruthven not been padding by with his tray and pulled the door open.

"Well, Melrose," began his aunt, who quickly disposed of him when she saw Richard Jury. "Superintendent! I didn't know you'd be here!"

"Nor did he know you'd be, so that makes three of us."

"But you told me about this little dinner, Melrose."

"Yes, but I didn't invite you, so what—?"

"Oh, that's all right. You're just forgetful. Lambert will be in directly. He's tying up his horse. He won't be staying for dinner. Just for a drink."

"That's just as well, we haven't enough of the hagfish to feed yet another uninvited guest."

"Hagfish?"

"Otherwise known as slime eels. They're a delicacy in South Korea, I understand. They're also known as the most disgusting marine animals. They emit slime—"

"How revolting! You can't be serious! I know you're lying, Melrose."

"Oh? Ruthven, ask Martha to step in, will you, and tell my aunt about dinner."

"Certainly, sir." With a little smile Ruthven swanned out of the room.

Melrose got Strether a whisky, as he looked to be on the verge of a seizure.

In another moment here was Martha, her usually snow-white apron smeared with something, Melrose guessed olive oil. He asked her to explain the main dish. Melrose knew Ruthven would have told her about the Agatha contretemps and Martha would have made preparations. "Yes, my lord? You wanted to know how the hagfish was coming along. Not much pleasure to prepare, it wasn't, but with a dusting of flour and a few dashes of salt, it doesn't look too bad."

Agatha, who had looked sick, looked sicker. "Never mind, Melrose. We neither of us will be staying."

"Oh, what a pity. So it'll just be the five of us, Martha, assuming that Mr. Trueblood and Miss Demorney are not put off by hagfish."

Martha curtsied and turned and left just as the doorbell rang, and Ruthven went off to answer.

Melrose heard the voices of Trueblood and Diane Demorney.

Trueblood wore a misty grey suit, muted tones of blue, green and yellow in shirt and tie, and looked like a Tahitian dawn. Diane was wearing white.

Hellos all round. "Agatha, old sweat, didn't expect to see you here, not with Melrose serving haggis."

How wonderful, Trueblood falling in without knowing what he was falling into.

"Hagfish, Marshall, not haggis."

"Sounds equally awful," said Diane, white making her black hair blacker.

"Couldn't agree more," said Strether, the uninvited. "We won't be staying."

"Ah," said Trueblood, drawing out the pitiful syllable. "Too bad."

"Oh, but we didn't tell you our news," said Agatha.

"Engaged? Married?" Melrose wanted to add "having a baby," but that might exceed the bounds of taste. Strether would have protested had he not been busying himself searching for the decanter.

Diane laughed a spray of vodka through her nose as Agatha looked furious.

"But that's usually what people mean," said Trueblood, "by 'our news.'"

"Mr. Trueblood, if you don't mind!" said Agatha.

"What's the news?" said Jury, the adult in the room.

Agatha simpered. "You mean Scotland *Yard* doesn't even know?"

She would drag this out as long as possible if someone didn't stop her. "None of us knows, Agatha. What is it?"

"A shooting."

"Who? Where?"

"Watermeadows."

"*What?*" Melrose surged from his chair.

"Yes. Miss Flood? That her name?" said Strether, still holding up his glass and waiting for the world to fill it.

Melrose gave him a lethal look. That such news should be delivered by such a person made him want to grab the poker. "Are you saying Miss Flood has been *shot?*"

It was clear neither of them knew what he or she was saying. Melrose still stood. Jury pushed him down. "Listen: you're staying here. I'll go to Watermeadows and let you know what's happened. But you stay here."

The doorbell rang again, and Ruthven ushered in Sydney Cooke.

Sydney looked around at the faces registering varying degrees of shock and took a step backwards. "Have I come at a bad time?"

Since Melrose could only sit there looking stupefied, Richard Jury went to Sydney.

"I'm so sorry, Miss Cooke. My name's Richard Jury. And you've walked in on a little village crisis. Not to worry, though. It'll all be resolved shortly. And as I, myself, am supposed to help out this resolution, I now must leave for a little while. In the meantime, Lord Ardry!"

Melrose saw that snap-out-of-it look and snapped out of it as Jury said good-bye and took his leave.

"Sydney. I'm so sorry . . . Let me introduce you." Which he did. "What will you have to drink?"

Sydney, not much of a drinker, said, "What do you have on offer?"

They all thought that very rich indeed.

10

As promised, Jury rang Melrose from Watermeadows:
"Now listen, friend: I'm giving you the bare bones; you will
wait on the details until I get back. Understood?"

"But—"

"Understood?"

"All right."

"Flora Flood was not shot. She's not the victim."

Melrose heaved a sigh of relief.

"She's the perp."

"Wha—"

"Flora Flood was the shooter. A man's dead. You're having dinner,
right?" When Melrose said yes, they were, Jury went on. "When you're
finished, see that everyone goes home. I'll be back straightaway and I
don't want to make a report in public."

"I'll be damned," said Melrose as he dropped the receiver, with a little thud, back in the cradle.

When he went back to the dining room, he faced a barrage of questions from everybody but Sydney Cooke, who was sitting on his right. "You know as much as I do, so feel free to fire away." He regretted the expression the moment it was out of his mouth.

It made no difference to his guests that Melrose could supply no details. The bare bones were enough to keep them talking away through the roast beef, the pudding, the cognac, the coats, the good-byes.

But Jury did not return straightaway; he was too busy soaking up the crime scene.

"She claims she didn't do it," said Ian Brierly, the DCI with the Northamptonshire police, "even though the gun was in her hand, according to the cook, who'd come through from the kitchen to find out what was going on, what all the disturbance was about." Brierly shrugged and flipped a notebook shut. "Go figure."

"I'd rather not have to. Is the identity of the victim equally ambiguous?"

Brierly grinned. "No. It's who she described as her soon-to-be ex-husband. Name of—" He flipped the notebook open again. "Servino. Tony Servino. Her story is that Servino turned up by surprise very angry over having received the divorce papers. Although they've been separated for nearly two years, according to her, and he knew he'd be served those papers very soon. Mad as a hornet, she said. Threatened her, yelled at her. Rolled up the papers and took a swing at her with them. She was scared and went to the desk where her uncle keeps a

.35 in a locked drawer—hardly adequate safety precautions, he'll find out—and aimed it at Servino, but not at his chest, more at his feet, as she just meant to back him off. Shot it, and that's where the shot came from. But someone—she claims someone else must have come in through the French door back there—" Brierly pointed his notebook at the glass doors behind him that were more or less in line with the body of the victim, only farther away "—and fired the shot that must have killed him, she claims."

"Another gun—"

"Well, that's the thing. It would have to have been another .35, which would be a hell of a coincidence. Because forensics is saying even before they dig the bullets from the floor and from the body, the casings are both .35s. No second gun has been found and no one saw anybody near the French door or anywhere else. Quite a yarn, right?"

Jury loved the old-fashioned Americanisms. He hadn't heard the word "yarn" since he was a kid. "It is, indeed." Jury looked toward the body. "Is that Dr. Keener doing the exam?"

"Yep. But hold off talking to him, will you, until we're done?"

"Absolutely. Sorry to be messing about in your crime scene, Ian. It's just that her next-door neighbor, Lord Ardry, is extremely anxious about her. We were about to have dinner when one of the guests said there'd been this shooting. I'll be off."

"No, no, I didn't mean for you to go. Look around as much as you want. Talk to the alleged shooter if you want, too. She's over there."

Jury saw Flora Flood, looking as if she were trying to disappear into the deep down-cushioned chair in which she sat, pressing a tissue to her eyes. One of many, for her lap was full of them.

"No; she looks too distressed to be talking to anyone except the man who's in charge, which would be you. I'll be going. Thanks, Ian."

Brierly walked with him to the door, saying, "Even just knowing what we do, I'd say her story sounds, well, fishy, wouldn't you?"

Fishy. Jury smiled. "I'd say it sounds impossible. 'Night."

And it was this fishy story that Jury relayed to Melrose when he got back to Ardry End, after making sure the dinner guests had left.

"Except for Sydney Cooke," said Melrose. "She's spending the night so she can check up on Aggrieved tomorrow."

Despite Jury's trying to convince him that he knew nothing else, no further details about the shooting, Melrose continued to press him for details.

"Husband? I didn't even know she was married."

"You don't really know Flora Flood very well, do you?"

"No, but still well enough to be pretty sure she didn't shoot him, even though her account of this sounds peculiar. But I expect anything's possible, isn't it?"

No, it isn't, Jury didn't say.

11

The next morning at Ardry End, after one of Martha's sumptuous breakfasts, Jury was drinking his third cup of coffee and admiring the Christmas tree. My Lord, where had these fabulous ornaments come from? The little owl, the horse and rider made to look as if they were following the hounds round the tree looked to Jury like Belleek china, they were so delicate and finely formed.

The front doorbell sounded and Jury heard Ruthven and the visitor, whose voice was familiar.

He walked into the foyer to find Tom Brownell. "Tom! What are you doing here? Not that I'm not glad to see you."

"Hello, Superintendent! I discovered Sydney was here seeing to a horse and just decided to barge in. I hope that's okay."

"Of course. Where is she, Ruthven?"

"She'll be in the stable, sir, seeing to Aggrieved."

Ruthven liked to say "stable," thinking it more befitting Ardry End than "barn," which it was. However, as it had been partitioned off for Aggrieved and Aghast, one could, Jury supposed, call it a stable.

"Let's go round the side," said Jury to Tom Brownell. "Thanks, Ruthven."

They found her forking hay into the holder in Aggrieved's part of the barn. The horse was eating oats and the very fact of his eating at all was testimony to Sydney's having helped him.

She looked wide-eyed at Tom and dropped the fork. "Grandad! Where'd you come from?"

"I went to the house, sweetheart, and your Aunt Ruthie told me you'd gone to Northampton to see to a sick horse. I drove here. How are you, Syd?"

Stiffly, Sydney met his embrace. There seemed to be a lot of ambivalence there. "I'm fine, Grandad." She broke away and went back to Aggrieved, smiling broadly at Jury. "Look how much better he is. Where's Mr. Plant?"

"He'll be back soon. Had to go into Northampton. He's going to be very happy about the horse."

"Much to my surprise," said Tom, "I ran into Mr. Jury here. I met him in Cornwall at the Old Success. You remember that inn?"

"Yes."

"Do you remember that friend of your mother, the one who nursed Gerald Summerston for a while before he died? Manon Vinet?" He told her what had happened.

"She's *dead*?"

He nodded. "I'm trying to work out why she was on the island. Did Daisy ever talk to you about her?"

She shook her head as Aggrieved moved from oats to hay. "Not much. I remember she said something about wanting to help her. Mum always loved Bryher . . . Sorry, Grandad."

She turned upon her grandfather the same concerned look she'd given to the horse. That, thought Jury, was probably a high compliment. Then she added, "Look, let's go where we can sit down. Mr. Blodgett told me I could always use his Florida room." That made her smile.

The three of them made their way to the hermitage and the sunporch Blodgett had added to the little stone structure. He had built it with his own hands, furnished it with wicker stuff that Trueblood had picked up at auction. With the sun high in the sky, it was pleasant.

After they sat down on the love seat and rocking chair, Tom asked her, "Help her how?"

"I don't know, but they had long conversations about something."

Tom said, thoughtfully, "I wonder if she could have had anything to do with your mother's death."

"Mum committed suicide."

"No, she didn't. Not Daisy."

"You don't know that, Grandad."

"But I do."

"You still think you can solve it, don't you?" Sydney turned on him with a force that astonished Jury. "You think you can save her. You just can't imagine you failed this time. Well, you did! She's dead!" But the look on Tom Brownell's face stopped her cold and she said, contritely, "I'm sorry, Grandad. I know how hard it was for you. But I think you just don't want to believe it."

This struck Jury as a complete misreading of Tom Brownell, to say nothing of its being a strangely defensive reaction. The man might not have wanted to believe his daughter killed herself, but that wouldn't have stood in the way of his objective judgment.

Jury heard a "Hullo" and saw Melrose Plant coming from the house towards the hermitage. "What are you all doing in the Florida room?" asked Melrose, then to Sydney, said, "I got the salve." He held up the small package.

"Aggrieved might not even need it. He's so much better."

Melrose looked toward the barn. The horse was now outside, munching grass. "You're a wonder-worker, Sydney."

Jury turned to Tom. "Here's the man after your own heart, Tom, the ex-Earl of Ardry."

"The man who jettisoned his titles? I'm delighted to meet you."

"Well, I *have* met you, Mr. Brownell."

"Where did we meet?"

"Right here." Melrose pulled a small book from his coat pocket. It was called quite simply *Brownell.*

"My God, I didn't think it was still around," said Tom.

"It's definitely around in our local book shop. According to the owner, when the book first came out it flew off the shelves. He had to keep reordering. His customers were fascinated. It's the recounting of a lot of your cases they liked, not too heavy on the technical details. It actually makes forensics both accessible and intriguing. What's astounding is how broad your knowledge is. You know things in so many different areas—"

"Grandad knows something about everything," said Sydney. "Except horses." She smiled.

"My favorite so far," said Melrose, "is the case about the drummer in the '90s band called 'Liftoff.' The drummer, Johnny Hamm, was found dead in the garage where he did his practicing. Drumsticks thrown against the wall, mixer overturned, speakers upended. A tape recorder was still playing. To the medical examiner, it was clearly suicide: he'd shot himself with the gun in his hand. The SOCO people, the forensics team agreed that all of it indicated suicide. Except Tom Brownell, who pointed out that the tape playing was of a concert that was the only one of Liftoff's failures, and that particular song was the only one Hamm had written that wasn't a smashing success. 'Johnny Hamm would never have killed himself while listening to that tape. Check it for prints.'

"They found several prints on the tape that belonged to Liftoff's former drummer, Earl Cooper. He'd been let go when Hamm came along. Cooper had been furious for years at Hamm for the loss of the job and his failure at getting a new one with another group. He had failed, of course, because he was a mediocre musician. You—" Melrose was looking at Tom now "—discovered Cooper had form for several incidents of violence, gave him high priority as a suspect. Cooper was finally arrested and found guilty of shooting Hamm. Cooper apparently found it ego-gratifying to play this piece of music. Dumb sod didn't realize it might point to him." Melrose shut the book. "That's pretty good, Tom."

"There's one case you won't find in there, Mr. Plant. My daughter's. I might have helped with the others, but Sydney's right, I couldn't save her."

Melrose looked down at the book again and looked back up at Tom Brownell. "Maybe you can save somebody else, though."

12

Jury did not recognize the old Aston Martin parked at the top of the Watermeadows drive. He parked Plant's Bentley behind it and went to the front door.

The door was opened not by Flora Flood but by the last person Jury expected to see: the old butler Crick.

Crick was no more wasted than he had been years before, yet wasting away he still seemed to be, as if having left yet another fuller outline of himself behind like a shadow on the walk.

If Crick was here, the Aston Martin—Jury glanced back over his shoulder—belonged to—

"Lady Summerston, Crick. Has she come back then?"

"Indeed, sir. Do come in."

Automatically, Jury's gaze traveled up the endless staircase, since he had never seen Eleanor Summerston anywhere but in her suite of rooms up there.

Crick said, "She'll be in the drawing room with Miss Flora, sir."

And so she was. They were seated side by side, Lady Summerston with her hand on Flora's shoulder, Flora with her own hands propping up her head.

Lady Summerston looked up in surprise and delight. "Superintendent Jury! Another terrible business," she said, as if welcoming him to the "terrible business." "Is there no end to the tragedy this poor house must endure?"

It was as if Watermeadows itself sat crumpled beside her, its head in its hands.

"I'm so sorry, Aunt Eleanor," said Flora. One would think that she, the hapless tenant, had brought it all down on their heads.

And had she? Jury wondered.

"Oh, please, my dear. I didn't mean—"

"I don't know what to do; I don't know—" Flora kept repeating this as she shook her head back and forth.

"Never mind. I'm sure Mr. Jury will set things right."

Mr. Jury wasn't. Thus, he was pleased if a little surprised to see Crick ushering Tom Brownell into the room.

Eleanor was up in a flash. "My dear Tom! How? Why? How did you ever get here? How did you hear—?" Finally she stopped asking herself questions and turned to Flora. "This is Tom Brownell, Flora—he's an absolute lifesaver. Now I know we'll be all right."

Tom said, smiling slightly, "Not quite yet, Eleanor."

Brownell must have felt every ounce of his success weighing him down, thought Jury. But his response did not dim Eleanor's smile, nor cast a shadow across the face of Flora Flood. Jury held out his hand to

Tom. "I think I agree with Lady Summerston. We'll be all right. Nice to see you again, Tom."

"Crick," said Eleanor, "could we have some tea, please?"

As Crick bowed and departed, she went on: "Tom, how do you come to be here?"

"Your next-door neighbor called me to tell me—but that's a long story," said Tom. "I met Superintendent Jury here at the Old Success. In Cornwall. It turned out that my granddaughter was at Mr. Plant's house seeing to his horse. She's a farrier. She lives in Bedfordshire."

"And what do police think, Tom?" She covered Flora's hand with her own.

"Police in general? Or just me?"

"You're not at odds, are you?" Eleanor looked from Tom to Jury and around the room as if there might be more policemen lurking.

Tom laughed briefly. "There are always odds, Eleanor."

"But you believe Flora—"

"Eleanor, I don't know anything beyond what Mr. Plant told me."

Flora interrupted. "Aunt Eleanor, this is what they know: My husband was shot. I had a gun. There appeared to be no one else in the room. If that's true, I shot him. How else would you read it?"

"Well, somehow else, Flora, since I know you didn't do it."

"But you don't. You just happen to believe me. Police don't happen to."

Eleanor said, "The man was a rotter. There must have been a dozen people with a motive to shoot him."

"'Must have been' isn't much of an option," said Tom.

"And why," put in Jury, "would someone follow him to Watermeadows to kill him?"

Jury watched Tom Brownell watching Flora Flood. Although Tom was sitting casually in his easy chair, his hand propping his chin, the scrutiny was intense.

Tom shifted his glance to Lady Summerston. "Eleanor, do you remember the woman who looked after Gerald for a short time when he was ill?"

"Yes. Manon Vinet. It was Gerald who spent time with her." Eleanor frowned. "I didn't much care for her. She was a very plausible person."

A word that Jury knew was seldom a compliment. "She had the appearance of credibility, you mean?"

"Oh, yes. The appearance of it. She was very good at putting herself in one's way. Manipulative."

"She must have put herself in the way of the wrong person, then," said Tom. "Her body was found on the sand at Bryher. She'd been shot."

"My God!" said Eleanor. "But who? Why? Have you any idea—"

"No. We haven't a clue as to why. I'm trying to build up a picture."

"I can help to fill it out: she was fond of men. I don't think you ever met my ward, Hannah Lean—" Here she looked quickly at Jury. "I'm sorry, Superintendent, to bring all that up—"

Jury was surprised that Lady Summerston had any idea that Hannah Lean's death was a personal loss to him. "That's all right, Lady Summerston."

Tom said, "I heard about her death, Eleanor. I'm very sorry."

"Yes, well, I bring it up because I suspected at one point there was something going on between this woman and Simon, Hannah's husband." She shrugged. "Simon was another man with an eye for women."

"By 'another' I assume you're referring to Flora's husband?"

"Yes. Tony Servino was quite the lady's man."

Flora said, "I think that's overstating it, Aunt Eleanor."

Tom turned to Flora. "Miss Flood, I wonder if we could have a word in private?"

Flora looked uncertain. "Why, yes, I suppose so." She gave her aunt a puzzled look and was met by one of reassurance from Lady Summerston. "Go ahead, Flora. Tom's a very fair person."

Jury wasn't sure what "fairness" had to do with it.

"And perhaps Superintendent Jury will join us." Tom motioned to Jury, who together with Tom followed Flora into a small room to the left of the entrance where Jury remembered waiting, several years earlier, for Crick to lead him upstairs to Lady Summerston. The portrait of Hannah Lean still hung at the top of these stairs. Jury looked away. Then, once inside the library, his eye followed a chain that led from the chandelier, which was no longer hanging but pulled back toward the bannister of a little balcony.

As they sat down, Tom said, "Perhaps you wouldn't mind going over what happened here last night. I know it's upsetting to have to keep repeating it, but I'd rather hear it from you than from the police. And incidentally, as I'm not currently with the police, you should feel under no obligation to talk to me at all. I'm merely helping out."

This little speech was delivered in Brownell's quiet and even tone, one that seemed to file away the hard edges of the experience.

Flora Flood told him. "It was just when we were starting dinner, around half past seven. Tony turned up and said he needed to talk to me and we went into the drawing room." She nodded to indicate the room they had just left. "He was really angry; he'd just got the papers about the divorce. I said I couldn't understand why he was so surprised as I'd told him I was filing for divorce. 'Only, not so soon,' he said. 'We've been separated for nearly two years, Tony. It's not soon.' He was fuming. He was becoming increasingly upset and told me he wouldn't sign any papers. When I told him he'd simply have to, he started toward me and I was scared. Tony could get very—physical. He was a threatening person to a lot of people. I backed away to the desk. My uncle keeps an automatic in the drawer. I took it out and aimed it at him. He kept coming toward me, so I pointed the gun at his leg and pulled the trigger. At the same time I heard something behind me and before I could look around, there was another shot and Tony crumpled to the floor. I went to him; I wasn't sure whether he was dead or alive. I ran back to the French door, where I'd heard the sound but there was no one there. It all happened so fast. Then the cook came in and Bub, who lives here, came in and the room seemed full of people." She looked away from him, into the drawing room and toward the French door, as if last night's intruder might reappear there.

Tom Brownell said nothing.

"I know it looks bad; but I didn't kill him. I wasn't shooting to kill. I just meant to scare him. Uncle Frank has a gun case in the mudroom off the kitchen. But it's always locked. Who on earth could have—?"

Apparently satisfied that she was finished with her account, Tom said, "Your husband, given your description of him, must have had enemies, or at least been much-disliked."

She nodded. "But not *that* much."

"So how would you explain this?"

"I can't, can—" Suddenly she looked up, toward the little balcony. She yelled, "Bub! Stop that!"

But Bub didn't stop, and the ones below ducked as if the chandelier were coming close to their heads, which it wasn't. Bub sailed above them but quickly lost momentum and he dropped down on the big sofa.

The chandelier was narrowed at each end and, with wires attached to the chain like rigging, looked more like a boat than a lighting device, oddly modern for a house of this age. Jury could see the temptation for a little kid.

"If it needs dusting or the lights need to be changed, the housekeeper pulls it in with a pole and ties it by its chain. I've told her not to leave it hooked to the bannister because Bub loves to take rides on it. I had the beam reinforced, but one day the ceiling will come down in bits and pieces."

"And who's this, then?" said Tom, looking at Bub.

"This is Bub, my husband's—" Her cough was tight, choked. "—little nephew." She reached out, shook him by the shoulder. "How many times do I have to tell you?"

Bub stood there looking shaken, until Tom Brownell said, "Come on over here, Bug; maybe you can help out."

"My name's not *Bug*, it's Bub." He seemed to think this error was rich with humor. But he went over to Tom.

"Oh, sorry."

"Are you a policeman?"

"No."

"Are you a detective?"

"No."

"Then what are you?"

"I'm not anything."

Bub appeared delighted that a grown person wasn't anything. "What do you do, then?"

"Ask little boys questions."

Bub liked that too.

Jury said, "Mr. Brownell was with Scotland Yard for many years."

"Did you catch bad people?"

"Sometimes."

"Did you ever shoot anyone?"

"Sure. Did you?"

"Me? I don't have a gun!"

"Were you upstairs last night when all of this happened?"

Bub nodded vigorously. "Me and Chester."

Tom looked around. "Where's Chester? Maybe he has a gun."

"Chester's my *dog*."

"Oh. And did you and Chester hear noises in the drawing room?"

"No." Bub shook his head hard.

Tom turned again to Flora. "Has your husband come here before?"

"No. We don't—didn't—really communicate. Which is what surprised me so much when he *did* come."

"Although it would seem to me not so surprising given he'd just been served divorce papers."

"But he knew they were coming."

"Perhaps he should've, only it sounds as if he didn't." Tom smiled to counteract this seeming contradiction of her account of her husband's state of mind. "Was there any particular reason why you did have these papers served now?"

"Well, no. I just thought it time, that's all. After all, we'd been apart for two years."

"I guess that's what I'm asking. Why did you wait so long? Did you just want to give the marriage more of a chance?" He was giving her the benefit of answering his own question.

"Another chance, yes."

Though that, thought Jury, would be difficult if they'd stopped talking to each other.

"Well, we won't bother you any longer, Flora. Bub."

"You're not bothering!" said Bub. But Tom was up by now.

Flora Flood said, "You hardly asked me any questions."

Tom smiled. "I might think of some more."

She seemed as reluctant as Bub to see him go.

"What did you think?" said Jury as they were getting into the car. He was surprised to discover Tom had walked from Ardry End. "Was she telling the truth?"

"I don't know. But he wasn't."

"He? You mean Bub?"

"He said he hadn't heard any noises coming from below. Yet he heard us talking at considerably less volume than she and her husband would have been."

"Why wouldn't he say so, then?"

"Because he's a kid, I expect. Kids always seem to think they're going to be in trouble if they admit to anything. The possibilities are endless when it comes to making mistakes that way."

It had started to rain and the defogger wasn't doing much to defog. Tom wiped the mist from inside the windscreen.

Jury said, "You don't think these cases are connected, do you? The one on Bryher and Flora Flood?"

Tom tossed the cloth on the floor of the car. "I don't know. Probably not. Though I do wonder at the Summerston connection. Do you mind?" he said as he took a pack of cigarettes from his pocket. When Jury shook his head, he lit one.

Tom said, "Did Brian exact a promise from you to go back?"

"Exact a promise? Macalvie doesn't do that. He just beats the living hell out of you if you don't."

Tom gave a snort of laughter. "He could be right."

"You're telling me to go back there?"

"I thought Brian Macalvie already did."

13

At breakfast the next morning, Jury asked Melrose if he wanted to accompany him to Bryher, to which Melrose responded that no, he didn't, as he needed to stay with Aggrieved.

"Why? Aggrieved has Sydney; he doesn't need you."

"You have Macalvie; you don't need me, either."

"Macalvie isn't going to Bryher; I'm doing it on my own."

"It's pretty unreasonable to expect you to go there all the way from Northamptonshire when he's right there in Exeter."

"Exeter isn't exactly 'right there.' It's a ninety-minute helicopter ride away."

"Well, it's a damned sight nearer the Scillies than Northants is."

"Do you two," said Tom Brownell, who'd stayed overnight along with his granddaughter, "usually argue like a couple of teenagers?"

"Pretty much," said Melrose. "Maybe you'd like to go with him to Bryher."

Tom looked out on the early day. "No. I'm going home with Sydney." He turned to Jury. "You going to do this all in one day?"

"Hope so. At least, I intend to."

The intention was fairly well borne out by the swiftness of his getting to Bryher that morning, first by plane from Heathrow to St. Mary's, via Cornwall Newquay, thence by the same boat that had ferried him and Macalvie two nights before to Bryher, where he was met once again by DCI Whitten.

"Actually, I think Commander Macalvie and his team pretty nearly bled them dry," said Whitten in answer to Jury's asking who he should interview at the Hell Bay Hotel, toward which they were headed in the jeep. "With the exception of this one waitress, Amy Dudgeon."

"Amy Dudgeon? Why wouldn't she have been bled along with the others?" Jury laughed.

"I got the impression that although she hadn't talked much to the victim, she knew something of a relationship between Manon Vinet and Dan Cooke."

"Daisy Cooke's husband?"

"Yes. We don't know there was one, of course. That's the point of the questions."

Except for a couple at one other table, the dining room at this time was empty, given it was well after lunch hour. Jury wasn't much of a lunch person anyway, but he was having a sandwich merely to employ the time of the waitress, Amy Dudgeon.

He made a few general comments to her about the peculiarity of what had happened on the beach two days before and, these not doing much to exact anything from her, turned to more specific comments, beginning with who he was. Backed up by his warrant card, that got her to sit down and look anxious.

"I hardly spoke to her at all," said Amy Dudgeon. "Hardly beyond taking her order and asking her if she wanted, like, coffee or tea. You know."

"I don't, Amy; that's why I'm asking. About Daisy Cooke's husband: I understand he left her."

"I don't know about *him* leaving *her*. What I heard was she told him to leave. Packed up his wheel and clay and took off suddenly."

"Wheel?"

"He was a potter." She picked up a small, swirly-colored vase. "His. He was good, I thought. He made these for all the tables." She studied it for a few moments, then returned it to the center of the table. "They were in here a few times for meals. He argued a lot. She didn't join in much. Argued mostly about here. I mean Bryher, not the hotel. He only wanted to leave. Well, it's not hard to understand. This place has nothing going on. Peace and quiet."

For which she seemed to have a burning contempt. Jury said, "But if you were a Londoner—"

"Don't I wish?" She laughed a little. "Funny he was the one wanted to travel, but she was the one always in Bewley's."

"Bewley's?"

"Little travel agency down there." She nodded toward the window. "Sorry, someone needs me." She got up and started toward the only other occupied table. A man had raised his hand to beckon her.

When he stopped in at Bewley Travel Lettings, Jury found a late-middle-aged woman behind a large wooden desk that held an old typewriter, on which she was typing at terrific speed. How long had it been since he had seen a typewriter being used at all, much less, speedily? *Josephine Bewley* (the name on a small brass plaque) did not even glance up when he entered, although he thought Bewley's might be grateful for the custom, as there was no one else in the place. Eventually, she raised her head, nodded and gestured for him to sit down in one of the two saddle-backed chairs arranged before her desk. She had sparse grey hair and was dressed in Liberty lawn.

Finally, she halted her fingers and said, "I'll be with you as soon as I'm free."

Free? Jury looked about him to see if he'd missed a few patrons eagerly awaiting her attention. But no. "Freedom" seemed to be part and parcel of the Bewley life. He sat and looked around the room. On the walls hung two or three obligatory views of the Scillies and one surprising shot of a maze, apparently at Hever Castle. But there one's travel plans would have to end. The rest of the area was hung with truly awful artwork, paintings whose subjects—owl, hare, human—shared expressions of surprise, their looks in a kind of stasis as if needing to react but hesitating, as if the paintings were about to sneeze.

Having placed her pen in its wooden holder, and letting her rimless glasses dangle on the black cord round her neck, the woman said, "Now, what can I do for you?"

Jury rose, took a step toward her desk and held out his warrant card.

She looked at it and said, "I've just had police round this morning. One visit should be sufficient."

He produced the photo of Flora Flood. "Have you ever seen this woman?"

"This is not the dead woman found on the beach." Her tone was accusing.

"No, it isn't. This woman is very much alive. But she's of interest in this case. We wonder if she was here."

"Here?" She actually pointed to the floor at their feet.

"No, I mean on Bryher."

Ms. Bewley, still a mite put out by this turn of events, said, "Only one time."

To which she added nothing as she opened a black ledger on the desk. The drama of but one sighting was lost on her.

Caught between surprise at this answer and the desire to throttle her, Jury said, "Where was 'one time'?"

Running her finger down the ledger columns she said, "At the Hell Bay." That was all.

"Ms. Bewley, could you tell me the exact circumstances?"

"Oh. Well, my brother and I were having dinner in the Hell Bay's dining room, the night's special being their excellent John Dory with shrimp." Her eyes caught his as if she were about to reveal something important. "And roasted squash."

Jury hoped the entire list of ingredients was not to follow.

"We were talking about the lack of custom of late. Surprising for this time of year . . ." On she went.

You asked for it, mate, thought Jury, as he sat down.

". . . sitting at a table alone."

His mind was so inhabited by the Bewley voice that he didn't even notice this was the period. End of account. Good-bye to the woman in the picture.

"Then?"

Blank look. "Ate her food, I expect. I wasn't waiting tables." She smirked, enjoying her little foray into humor.

"Of course not, but this woman at some point must have moved."

"Not until the man sat down." Eyes dropped to the ledger again.

Silence. Jury did not know where he came by the control that held him to his chair. "The man?"

"I've no idea who he was."

"No, but perhaps you could describe him?"

"Describe?"

This novel idea held her attention until someone walked into the room, not from outside but from a door at the back, nodded pleasantly to Jury and said, "Hullo, I'm the other half of the Bewley business." He extended his hand. "Matthew Bewley, Josephine's brother."

Jury shook the hand as he produced his warrant card and the picture of Flora Flood once again. "I understand from your sister here that you saw her at the Hell Bay, in the dining room."

Matthew was as direct as she was indirect, as full of detail about the right things as she was about the wrong, as willing to accede as she was to obstruct.

"Indeed. We were there for dinner and sat at a table not far from hers. She was joined as she was eating by a youngish man—well, young-ish to me, as I'm now oldish—"

Josephine interrupted. "Don't be silly, Matthew. You look ten years younger than you are."

"But that depends on what I am." He smiled at Jury. "I'd never seen either of them before, so I can't help you out much. He was tall-ish, dark, not very handsome. Good clothes, though. He kept his coat on . . ." Matthew looked puzzled, as if he were trying to work this out. "I got the impression he was not there to meet this woman, but had happened on her by chance, if you know what I mean."

Jury nodded, as Josephine interrupted: "How did you ever come by that notion? Just seeing them for a moment or two?"

Matthew Bewley didn't bother answering, but asked his own question of Jury: "What's your interest in her, Superintendent? Has it got to do with this dead woman on the beach?"

"Very possibly." Jury paused. "I was wondering about Daisy Cooke's death. There seems to be some question as to whether it was suicide or accidental."

After a few moments of contemplation, Matthew said, "I know one shouldn't speak of a suicidal 'type,' as there is no type."

"You're suggesting Daisy Cooke would not be the type, if there were one."

"Absolutely. Daisy, although in what I thought to be a despairing situation, would never have acceded to it. She'd switch her beleaguered hand to something else."

"Beleaguered hand? Mr. Bewley, you've lost me."

"Like a poker player: 'I'll play you another hand, but only with a fresh deck.'"

"The fresh deck being—?"

"Another way of looking at the situation."

Jury smiled. "I like your cryptic language, but I'm having trouble with this metaphor."

Matthew *tch-tch*'d. "And you a CID superintendent. What I mean is that Daisy Cooke wasn't the type either to give in or to get out without a fight. And by 'fight' I mean some tough thinking. Daisy thought things through. Ouch! *Th, th, th*. Three *th* sounds in a row. I'd make a lousy poet."

Jury smiled. "Or a really good one. So what was her despairing situation, the one she wouldn't give in to?"

"Dan Cooke, is what I'd say," offered Josephine, who, having put by her ledger, was now typing up something on the ancient machine and not stopping in order to comment.

The interruption didn't throw off her brother, who was probably used to her answering his questions for him. "Her marriage. Not that there was anything wrong with Dan as such, but he hated living on Bryher, and Daisy loved it. Temperamentally, they were worlds apart. She liked solitude, silence, nature—and, of course, her mother was here."

"Real sick was Mrs. Brownell. Cancer, I think," said Josephine. "Poor woman."

"So Daisy wouldn't leave her mother, that it?"

"Yes."

"But couldn't she have left after her mother died?"

"Daisy felt tied to the place after that. She wouldn't have left Bryher."

"If her husband hated living here, why didn't they just separate?"

Matthew shrugged. "I imagine they would've eventually. For all of that, it would never, never have driven Daisy Cooke to kill herself."

"But perhaps there was something else, something people didn't know about that had trapped her."

Matthew smiled and nodded toward the wall of art: "See that picture of Hever Castle? That's the water maze. Daisy loved to look at that. I said, 'You'd get damned wet, wouldn't you, working your way out? If you could get out.'

"'There's always a way out,' she said. That was Daisy. She'd've found a way."

"Did you know the Summerstons, Mr. Bewley? They spent a number of holidays here, I understand."

"Saw them. I didn't know them, no. But you might want to have a word with Jack Couch. I'm pretty sure he knew Mr. Summerston. Sir Gerald, was he?"

"Yes. Where would I find Mr. Couch?"

"Right along there." Matthew Bewley was at the door now, pointing off to his right. "Just past the Bryher shop. Before the quay. Anyone can tell you."

"Thanks."

Jury tapped at the glass door, which was open a couple of inches. "Mr. Couch?" he called out.

A thin, wiry man came through from another room, opened the door and said, "That's me. What can I do for you?"

Jury had his ID out and brought it up to eye level. "Sorry to bother you, but—"

"Scotland Yard? Who was this woman, anyway, that had them sending in the big guns?"

Jury eyed the shotgun mounted on the wall. "That a Winchester, Mr. Couch?"

He smiled. "It is indeed, only this didn't shoot her."

Jury returned the smile. "And that's not why I'm here."

"Good. Come on back with me, will you, I want to finish cleaning a rifle back here."

He led Jury through a small dining room into a smaller room that was lined with cabinets and had in its center a table with a gun clamp that held a rifle. Jury looked around at the cabinets. "Guns?"

"I collect them. Believe me, they're all registered. And I keep it locked up in here tight as a drum. Kids love the place, so I have to be doubly careful."

"You have children here?"

"Not to worry, they never get their hands on any of them. And to make up for it, I give gun talks. I tell them, if they want to visit the house, they have to come to the talks."

Jury smiled. "Lectures?"

"You bet: the danger of guns. They have to memorize a few rules, too."

"You must be popular with the kids around here. Do you know Zoe and Zillah Noyes?"

"Zoe? My Lord, yes. She's one of the best listeners. Always in the audience. Also, she's got a gun I wouldn't mind owning. Oh, don't look like that. Zoe hasn't got it in her sock drawer. Her aunt keeps it locked up. It's an old SIG Sauer P226. Wouldn't shoot outside of the box, anyway. Doubt it's been cleaned in years." Jack pushed a white plastic tube into the barrel of his rifle. "So what do you want to know, Superintendent?"

"Are you familiar with the Summerstons, who sometimes visited Bryher, specifically Gerald Summerston? Matthew Bewley said he thought you knew him."

Jack looked up, drawing the long rod out of the bore guide. "Not very well, but we did talk some, yeah. Korean War. He got a Queen's award for bravery, he told me."

"Conspicuous Gallantry award. Korea. You're interested in the Korean War?"

"Interested in all of them. But especially that one."

"You're familiar with the Battle of the Imjin River?"

"Who isn't?" Jack Couch laughed. "It was huge. I wasn't in it, I mean, I wasn't in Korea. I was in the Falklands. Had a lot of friends in the service. My dad was at Imjin. I more or less grew up in the service. My dad—now there was a hero! Dad got the Military Cross. A real bona fide hero." He looked away from the rifle, out through the window. "He told me not to brag about it. Poor form." Jack smiled.

"As opposed, perhaps, to Gerald Summerston?"

Jack turned back to the gun barrel. He drew the cleaning rod back and forth. "You could say that. Thing is, my dad never talked about the medal. Never. Neither did the men who'd been with him. But Summerston brought up that battle a lot in conversation. Pretended sometimes to play it down."

"Did you have any thoughts about his part in it? The award?"

Jack shrugged. "I questioned what the man said, that's all. Probably because of my own father being the sort of man he was."

Jury got up. "Well, I won't bother you further, Mr. Couch."

"Jack, please. And it's no bother. You haven't said if police have solved this one, though."

Jury shook his head. "Not yet."

Leaving Hell Bay to its frenzied waters, Jury sat in the bar of the Old Success talking on his mobile to Brian Macalvie.

"Did you work Daisy Cooke's death?" asked Jury.

"Me? No. Brownell did most of the work."

"But he was the Met. And she was his daughter. He wouldn't have been the principal here."

"No. The case actually belonged to a Superintendent—Smithson, as I recall."

"Everyone saw it as a suicide?"

"Everybody except Brownell himself, even though the medical examiner found enough prescription drugs in her system to kill her."

"What about you? You agreed with that verdict?"

"No. Daisy Brownell was the most together person I ever met in my life, I mean like a rock. I can understand why Tom couldn't believe suicide. And frankly, I couldn't imagine Daisy being blindsided—which is kind of what suicide is, don't you think?" said Macalvie.

"Not really. It's too complex to be a sudden, event-altering thing. And in her case, what was the blind side?"

"No one knew for sure, but the guess was it was Dan Cooke, her husband."

"But she solved that problem, in the sense she took action. Apparently, she told him to leave. Another woman might have just wrung her hands and hung on. But Daisy took action. She just doesn't sound the sort to see herself as a victim, or see a situation as hopeless." Jury took a drink of his Adnams, and repeated what Matthew Bewley had told him about Daisy's verdict on Hever Castle's maze: "'There's always a way out.' That doesn't sound like a woman who'd kill herself."

On his way to the airport, Jury got a call from DCI Brierly.

"We may have turned up a motive in the Servino case."

"What?"

"That the car crash that left her partly paralyzed wasn't really an accident."

"If that were true—that she hated him enough to shoot him— would she have waited five years?"

"No, unless she found out something new about it. Tony Servino loved cars. He was always taking the Alfa Romeo out over different kinds of roads at different speeds. And he liked tinkering with them."

"And this particular tinker was what?"

"Removing one of the supports from under the bonnet. Which would make the car even more vulnerable in any kind of collision."

"But for the driver too, surely. You're saying Servino would risk his own life to kill her?"

"He risked getting hurt, yes. But he knew all the roads and every obstacle along them. The guy could have practiced for a long time. He knew how hard to hit that barrier. If it didn't work, he could always try again. And don't forget, no one would think it was attempted murder, not certainly by the driver of the car."

"So how did this come to light recently?"

"The mechanic at an auto repair shop that specializes in foreign cars. Italian, mostly: Maserati, Alfa Romeo, Ferrari. You know."

"No, I don't. So what did he—who was this, anyway?"

"Name's Crenshaw. He owns the place—Crenshaw's Foreign Cars—just off the North Circular Road. It's where Tony Servino bought the car. Crenshaw sells used cars—but only the ones in top condition—"

"Of course. Go on."

"He didn't think anything of it at the time—this was years ago, they bought the car—but then when he happened to read about the accident—it got some play in the London papers—he started to wonder a little. There's record that he called police about it a month or so after the accident."

"About what?"

"All of the interest in this car and what would happen in a collision. Maybe you should talk to him. He was kind of vague, trying to remember the details."

"You got a number for this Crenshaw?"

"Sure. Alex Crenshaw." Brierly gave Jury the number and repeated the location.

"Thanks, Ian. Hold it. Hasn't Flora Flood been charged yet?"

"No. She's got one hell of a legal team. Treadwell—"

"That's Melrose Plant's firm, I think. Best in London."

"She'll need the best," said Brierly, ringing off.

When he was some ten miles from Long Piddleton, Jury called Ardry End and asked Ruthven if Melrose was there, or—

"At the Jack and Hammer, Superintendent, although he should be back shortly."

Knowing "shortly" could mean a lot of things, Jury thanked Ruthven and told him he'd be at Ardry End "shortly" but that he thought he'd check the Jack and Hammer first.

14

Which Jury was now entering—or trying to, as the door was blocked by Dick Scroggs, whose broad back Jury was trying to maneuver around, and Mrs. Withersby, standing in front of Dick, holding something.

"Shoot, Withers!"

The voice was Trueblood's and the "something" looked like a kid's water gun. Jury got a small spray on his neck. "What the hell's going on?" He edged past the two and saw Trueblood some ten feet away, also holding some gun-like thing that delivered its peanut-bullet to Scroggs's shoulder—or slightly past it—and then another to the molding of the door.

Behind Trueblood was a large cardboard cutout, roughly drawn as a double door. Joanna Lewes was holding it steady.

"Richard!" called Vivian Rivington, who, along with Diane Demorney, served as audience.

"What's going on?" Jury asked again.

Trueblood answered: "A reenactment of the crime scene. Clever, isn't it?"

"No," said Jury, taking the chair beside Vivian. "What's that alleged gun you're using?"

"It fires peanuts. Picked it up at Windsor from a lad who was on a tour who held me up for ten quid."

"I'm done. Where's my gin?" Mrs. Withersby moved toward the public bar where Dick Scroggs was shoving a glass under one of the optics.

"You wasn't supposed to wet me, Withersby."

"Where's Plant? Ruthven told me he was here. I'm amazed he isn't part of this tableau."

"Just left ten minutes before you came," said Trueblood.

"I think Marshall's been rather clever," said Diane, who then called to Dick for another drink. "Really, drinks all around," she added.

"I hate to say it," said Marshall Trueblood, who didn't hate to say it at all, "but that 'intruder' business is a bit of a cliché, isn't it?"

"Cliché?" said Joanna Lewes, who had stopped being the French door to come and sit down.

"There's always an intruder. You should know that; you've written enough books."

Joanna said, "It isn't a *story*, Marshall; someone was shot to death. That really happened."

"But the rest of it could be exactly that: a story, like the intruder bit," said Trueblood, wiping a spot from his gun.

"You think she was lying?" said Vivian. "And she killed him?"

"That's the alternative to the intruder story, isn't it?"

Vivian said, "We don't have enough facts to draw a conclusion. What would her motive have been, for instance?"

"He was her husband," said Diane Demorney.

"Her husband? That's a motive in and of itself?"

"Considering the ones I've had, I'd say so."

Trueblood said, "Look, Dick Scroggs is two heads at least taller than Withersby. Tony Servino was tall. Flora Flood is rather short. Now, if you're trying to shoot Servino and she's standing in front of him, why not go for a head shot? Much easier target for this alleged intruder. He aimed for the torso, the chest, supposedly. Aiming at the chest, he would have had to go through Miss Flood." He looked around the table. "If you take my meaning, for God's sakes."

Jury said, "I take it. Flora Flood was the target, not her husband."

"Good for you."

"Well, I am with the Met. And where'd you get the details of this crime?"

"From Melrose, who got them from you and DCI Brierly."

"Brierly wouldn't be giving out—"

The crime scene charade was followed by Jury's mobile vibrating in his pocket. It was Macalvie.

"You're in Northants already? Come to Exeter."

"Macalvie, I just left."

"So? Come back. There's a cathedral here."

"Northampton has one too."

"Not with a murder in it."

Jury was silent.

"You still there?"

"No."

"Oh, come on. You must be curious. Young woman found shot in Exeter Cathedral."

"*In* the cathedral? Where?"

"In the nave. If you can beat that—"

"I can't. But why call me?"

"You'll see."

"*What* will I see?"

"It's the third one."

Jury frowned. "You're not making sense. third one what?"

"Don't be dense. Murder. Shooting."

Jury thought for a moment. "If you're referring to Bryher and Manon Vinet, I believe I count *one* shooting."

Trueblood seemed to have heard enough to raise his perfect eyebrows.

As if defending himself against the eyebrows rather than Macalvie's theory, Jury said, "That's ridiculously tenuous, Macalvie—"

"God, but I hate that word."

"There's nothing to connect the three, Macalvie, certainly not geography: Bryher, Northampton, Exeter. And if you check around, I bet you find a few more shootings in the same time frame."

"I did. Six. Five men and an old gran shot in a break-in."

"And?"

"Just grab Tom Brownell and get over here."

"Why in hell would he want to go to all the way to Exeter?"

"Because he's Tom Brownell." Macalvie rang off.

Jury stared at the dead mobile and looked up.

Only to be targeted by four pairs of eyes around the window-seat table. Staring.

"What?" he said.

15

"You just missed him," said Melrose in answer to Jury's question about the whereabouts of Tom Brownell. "He left for the farm not ten minutes ago."

"Hell," said Jury. "Did he go with Sydney?"

"No. She's still here."

"Why weren't you in your usual chair at the Jack and Hammer?" He sighed. "Me, I'm really worried about Flora Flood."

"Well, Trueblood's theory might worry you even more."

"It worries me that Trueblood *has* a theory. What is it?"

"That she was the target, not her ex-husband."

That made Melrose's eyes widen and got him to put down his glass. "How does he come up with that?"

Jury explained the relative positions of the two, including Mrs. Withersby's part in the little drama.

Melrose laughed in spite of himself, said, "Does this make it even more baffling?"

"Could it be? I got a call from Brian Macalvie." He told Melrose about that.

"The cathedral?"

Jury nodded. "I expect I'll be going to Exeter tomorrow."

"But Richard . . . you don't really think there's something to this theory?"

"No. Except Macalvie thinks there's some connection."

"But this depends on Marshall's being *right* about Flora as the real target. I hate to think that. Did Macalvie come up with any motive in this cathedral shooting?"

Jury shook his head. "Not yet."

Melrose slid down in his chair. "Oh, surely these are three random shootings. 'Serial killer'? Cornwall, Devon and—over three hundred kilometers away—Northants? There's got to be some other connection—if there's any connection at all—between these three shootings. I mean, just look at the difficulty of access to two of them: the island of Bryher can be reached only by boat, and Watermeadows is a private estate outside of a little village in Northamptonshire. It makes no sense unless the three people were specifically targeted. And that still isn't to say whether one of the three was Tony Servino or Flora Flood."

"I agree. All the same, this new shooting does make me wonder."

"Wonder away. But don't go to Exeter to do it."

"Did Tom leave any number? I don't have his mobile number."

Melrose frowned. "Why?"

"Because I want to call him, obviously."

Melrose's frown deepened as he rose and grasped the silk bellpull near the mantel.

Ruthven was there even as the bellpull floated back against the wall.

"He did indeed m'lord," said Ruthven in answer to the question about the mobile number. He moved to a desk at the end of the room and brought back a small metal address book, clicked it open and handed it to Melrose.

"Excellent, Ruthven. Surely you're not thinking of driving to Exeter tomorrow morning? You just now got back."

"Surely, I am. Macalvie wants Tom, too."

"Well, if you insist on this hectic drive—nearly three hours it'll take you from here—at least take the Bentley. It's a bit faster than that police-issue thing."

"I couldn't—"

"Oh, yes, you could. Ruthven." Melrose nodded at Ruthven.

Who went immediately to another room, returned and put the keys in Jury's hand.

16

Tom Brownell didn't have to be persuaded to go to Exeter after Jury told him about Macalvie's phone call.

"Serial killer?" said Tom, as they drove a nearly trafficless M4 towards Devon. "I'd say that's ridiculous."

"I agree. But he's come up with a few ideas over the years that struck me as impossible. They weren't. Do you know Dennis Dench?"

"Forensic anthropologist? Sure. He's brilliant."

"Macalvie once argued that the bones under study belonged to a certain boy, a murder victim. Denny said no, the kid would have been, or the bones were, too young."

"And Brian was right."

"Of course. He always is."

"It's some kind of, I don't know—imaginative grasp. Some combination of intuition and reasoning. I wish I had it."

"You? Come on, Tom, no one's got a better grasp—"

"But not intuitive. I go almost solely by pure reason."

"So it's you, Macalvie and me—what are we? The three wise men?"

"It's the season for it, isn't it?"

The nave of Exeter Cathedral was the longest medieval nave in the world. Jury stood with Tom Brownell, looking at the vaulted ceiling.

"The acoustics in this cathedral are so incredible I'd think a shot would have careened off these walls and that ceiling," said Jury.

"Fireworks," said Macalvie.

"What?"

"There were fireworks. Not in the cathedral grounds, of course, but out there—" Macalvie jerked his thumb over his shoulder. "The city decided to allow a little pre-Christmas celebration. Only for about half an hour. Could have muffled a shot."

"So I expect it *was* opportunistic," said Tom.

"The shooter might have followed the fireworks, but how could he have followed the woman?" said Jury. "Unless he knew that—"

"That she was a regular, so to speak. And she was, according to the ladies I talked to. Very devout. Came here several evenings a week," said Macalvie, "in addition to other times."

"He knew she'd be here. But that means he was looking for her, not some random target. That doesn't sound like a serial killer."

As the three stood in the nave, Macalvie outlined it for them.

"First, serial killings often look crazily unrelated—or even crazily related: it's the craziness that counts. Remember that case you had where all three victims wore designer shoes—?"

"That wasn't a serial killing, Macalvie."

"I know. But it had the appearance of one because of the shoes and the escort services. I'm talking about appearance here."

"There's still the constraint of geography. Here we're dealing with three different counties. And one of them's Northants. Devon and Cornwall are close together. But Northamptonshire? Come on," said Jury.

"Manon Vinet knew Daisy, and probably Flora Flood. Daisy possibly knew Flora. But now we have a fourth woman who seems completely unrelated to the other three."

"Except she wasn't unrelated."

"How do you work that out, Brian?"

"Moira Quinn was a maid for the Summerstons for a time. Her mother was the cook at Summerplace and got her the position."

Jury looked up. "So you think she knew Manon?"

"Could be. It's a connection nonetheless."

"You have my attention. Where was the body found?"

Macalvie nodded toward a point farther down the nave. "Down there. Fifth bay, near the misericords."

They walked toward the east, Tom commenting, "That glorious east window."

"Fourteenth-century glass," said Macalvie. "They dismantled it during the war, took out all the panes to keep them from being shattered."

"I can understand why."

They came to the place where the now-absent body was still outlined.

"Moira Quinn," said Macalvie. "Aged 38, lived with her mum in a flat on the Quay; worked at Debenhams as a cleaner. Here, as a matter of fact, as a holy duster."

Tom Brownell looked a question.

"Just what it says. Donate their time to clean in the cathedral. I spoke to a couple of the ladies who work here. They said she was very, very good at it. And very devout. Said Moira used to live in London—Battersea, also with her mum. Worked in South Ken, Belgravia, Docklands, also cleaning. Mum's destroyed, as the Irish put it."

"I'm sure the Irish are right," said Tom.

17

The woman who opened the door to them was small, dark-haired, blue-eyed and inconsolable. That was clear to Jury even though her face was perfectly free of tears, and nor was there a sign of a recent bout of them. It was the way her gaze was fixed on Jury—

But then it shifted to Tom Brownell, who said, "Mrs. Quinn, forgive us for bothering you. We're police—"

That voice that could melt ice caps.

Her head and her body moved sideways and she leaned against the doorjamb.

For a moment, Tom did not disturb this position. The next minute he put his hand on her shoulder. "May we go in, Mrs. Quinn?"

She moved then and turned back to them as if she had been Betsy Quinn, good hostess, all along, stretched her arm to motion them into a room with an unlit fireplace—unlit but not unlaid—and indicated an easy chair on either side of it. She herself took a seat on the small cream-linen sofa facing the fireplace.

Tom said nothing, looking at Jury to start the questioning.

He did. "Mrs. Quinn, we know it's very hard for you right now, but it's important to us to ask you about your daughter. You see, there's at least one other death that appears to touch on Moira's own."

"You mean that French nurse that worked at Summerplace when Moira was there. She had a funny name, French for Madeline, my Moira said. I don't know much about her, but—"

Jury held up his hand. "No, no. It's Moira we wanted to know about."

"Who would ever do such a thing? The dear lass." She looked down at her overlapped hands.

Jury said, "That's what we were hoping you might help us with. Had Moira been having trouble with anyone in particular? A man, perhaps?"

Betsy Quinn looked from Jury to Tom, eyes wide, as if in surprise. "You think it was Moira they meant to kill? Oh, surely not. Surely the killer was just a bad shot."

Jury and Tom exchanged a glance. Then Tom said, "I don't quite take your meaning, Mrs. Quinn."

"Well, it must have been the other girl."

"What other girl?"

"Not 'girl,' either of them. But the other holy duster. She usually worked beside Moira. Name's—Glynis something. And the ladies said she was there, too."

Jury, already lost, was lost again. "The ladies?"

"The embroiderers, the Holy Dusters. You know."

Holy Dusters. Embroiderers. The secular seemed more and more swallowed up by myth. Or at least the mundane overtaken by metaphor. All Jury could think of was *Heart of Darkness*, with the little woman sitting by the entranceway knitting black wool.

But Tom Brownell, once surprised, refused to be surprised again, and said, calmly, "So you're saying that this other woman is the one the shooter aimed to hit and he shot Moira by mistake? I'm sorry to put it that way, but that is what you mean, isn't it?" When Betsy Quinn nodded sadly, Tom said, "But do you know why anyone would want to shoot her?"

"No. No more than someone would want to shoot my Moira."

"Mrs. Quinn," said Jury, "your Moira got that job with the Summerstons because you were their cook, right? And you knew they were looking for someone to take care of Gerald Summerston?" He thought that sounded better than "wanted another maid."

She nodded, the handkerchief still bundled against her mouth.

"Well, if you'll pardon me for going off in a slightly different direction, it's important to the case if you can recall anything about other members of the staff, and their relationship to your employers." He was putting this very poorly, and looked at Tom.

"What we mean is, whether they got along as well as you did with Lady Summerston. Of you, she speaks very highly indeed. She says no cook she's tried since can begin to measure up."

At this, Betsy Quinn dropped the balled-up handkerchief in her lap and managed a tiny smile. "Yes, it's true, she did like my cooking. But your question was . . . ?"

Tom said, "Whether she thought as highly of other staff members. Whether she had problems with them. Whether there was something going on in the house."

Betsy frowned and was silent.

Tom rose. "We're sorry, Mrs. Quinn, to have intruded at a time like this. Perhaps we could come back—"

But Betsy, having been called away for a few moments from the pain of the loss of her daughter, preferred to be called away longer; also, there was the question of "something going on in the house" to intrigue her. And the company of these two men, even though they were police. The woman obviously needed a little company. There seemed to be no one else.

"No, no. That's all right. Please sit down. You're saying—?"

"Asking," said Jury, "more than saying. In your position, you'd have been the most likely person to have heard, well . . . rumors or simple gossip about the behavior of, say, one or another of the maids?"

She sat back. "Oh. Now, I wouldn't want to—"

"Believe us, Betsy, nothing you say about anyone will go beyond these walls," said Tom.

"We're simply trying to work out how all of this, how what went on at that house could have affected your Moira."

"I remember," said Betsy, "there was trouble with the housemaid, Anna."

"What kind of trouble?"

"Mr. Gerald."

Jury was surprised by the directness of this answer. "You mean something going on between the housemaid and Gerald Summerston?"

"Yes."

Tom said, "Had she shown a little too much interest in him? Was that it?"

"Or the other way round," said Betsy.

"So she was dismissed."

"She went, and I think that's why. It's too bad, isn't it, that the servants have to pay a price for what their supposed 'betters' have done?"

"It certainly is, Mrs. Quinn," said Tom. "So then your daughter would have replaced the housemaid, right?"

"Not that one. The one who followed."

"You're not saying that she, too—"

"Oh, no. She quit on her own. Edith. It was Edith that Moira replaced."

Tom leaned closer to her. "And Moira, herself?"

"Did she have trouble?" Betsy smiled tightly. "Oh, no. Moira was much too smart for that." Betsy seemed puzzled. "Anyway, she decided to leave. She was a little sick for a while. But then she got herself a job at Debenhams."

Jury liked it that a department store beat out Gerald Summerston.

But he wasn't sure he believed it. And nor did Tom, who said, "Seems unlikely that someone as pretty as Moira Quinn wouldn't have been pursued by a man who couldn't seem to keep his hands off any woman he fancied."

"I agree. And the fact that Moira was murdered along with Manon Vinet makes me wonder even more. Have you seen her medical records?"

"No. I don't know if they've been found yet. Why?"

"She was a little sick after she left. I bet it wasn't flu."

18

On their way back, Jury and Tom stopped at a Welcome Break along the M4, collected some soup and salad in the food court and sat down in a booth.

Jury brought up Sydney's treatment of Aggrieved. "She's really good. She seems to have an affinity for horses that's almost—mystical. I don't know why I chose that word."

"Because you're too polite to say 'obsessive.' She certainly likes your friend, the ex-lord. He knows something about horses, does he?"

"Nothing at all. You told me that she'd talk only to someone who did, so I told him to bone up, and I expect he learned enough to convince her."

Tom laughed and spooned up his soup. "Why don't they know how to make tomato soup anymore?" He replaced the spoon on the plate. "Too acidic."

Jury smiled. He had an idea Brownell analyzed everything that came his way.

"Mind if I smoke?" said Tom.

Yes. "No," said Jury. "What is it you think Sydney knows, Tom?"

Tom had lit his cigarette and was blowing a stream of smoke away from Jury. "Perhaps something about Daisy's death. I wish I could get her to talk to me, but she won't. I expect I don't know enough about horses."

Jury thought for a moment. "I might. I mean, know somebody. He's connected with a stud farm in Cambridge."

"Owner? Trainer?"

"Investments."

"If there's one thing Sydney's not interested in, it's investing."

Jury shook his head. "Of course. Only, this fellow's the stepson of the owner and he knows a lot about horses. I mean a *lot*. And about people, too."

Tom was thoughtful. "Sydney seems to think people who do are on her wavelength."

"Maybe I can get him to visit Ardry End."

The long, winding drive up to the front of Heron House curved past the stable within which dull gold light threw the shadow of someone across the wide sill.

"That must be John Ridgely. He's stable master and general dogsbody, I guess. Slow down, Richard."

Jury slowed to a stop as Tom called out, "Ridge. Why're you here at this godforsasken hour?"

"Just to check on things. Couldn't sleep."

"Where's Sydney?"

"Up at the house. She was here for a few minutes. Saw my truck and thought something was up with one of the horses."

"But everything's okay?"

"Absolutely."

Tom said goodnight and raised the car window, and they drove on. "I don't much care for it that he's over here whenever he feels like it."

"Something to do with Sydney?" said Jury.

"A lot to do with Sydney, if you ask me."

Jury didn't question him. In another two minutes they were at the front door.

"Front door" was an inadequate description of this Scarlett O'Hara entrance of vermillion, a wood one was not used to seeing, certainly not in a door. Jury had picked up his wood-knowledge from a forensic botanist in the art squad who had inspected a picture frame for him.

"Magnificent house, Tom."

"I hate it. All show, no substance."

Jury had never thought of any house as "substantive." But why not? Home meant substance to many people.

The door was opened by a small, sad-seeming maid who looked fallen as a leaf—drifted. Strewn, rather than just standing there. Where had this strange image come from?

From the cathedral. Standing in the square with the trees blowing in the crosswind that had chilled them.

"I'm sorry, Sadie," said Tom, "to drag you out here. I forgot my key."

"Oh, it's quite all right, sir; I was in the kitchen anyway, heating up milk for cocoa. Would you care for some? Or tea?"

"No, no, thank you, Sadie. We'll just sit in the study for a while. Never mind about us."

It looked as if she would mind all over the place; it looked as if she could think of nothing she'd rather do than mind Tom Brownell. But she drifted off, leaf-like.

They went into a fire-warmed room with pale blue walls and soft leather chairs. Jury sat down as Tom went to a drinks table and came back with two whiskies.

"Daisy died of an overdose, I understand. Of what?"

"Pain meds. I never could figure out why she had the tablets."

"Tablets. You could hardly overdose on *those* accidentally. You'd have to take too many to do the job."

"There were also traces of an antidepressant."

"What was she depressed about?"

"Her marriage? Dan Cooke wasn't much of a husband. I don't think it ever got through to him that he'd married the girl." Tom laughed, bitterly.

"Was he there in the house? I mean when she took—?"

"No. That's probably true, given he spent most of his weekends in the city and the boatman hadn't seen him. He hadn't been ferried over from St. Mary's." Tom paused. "You're not thinking he killed her?"

"I'm thinking somebody did."

Tom rose and went to the fireplace, took the poker and shoved a sparking log back on the pile. "Daisy murdered? That's preposterous."

"No more than suicide. That picture of Daisy is all wrong, given what I've heard about her. She was like you, Tom; she was a problem-solver."

Tom reseated himself, picked up his glass and said, "That was a problem I certainly didn't solve." He paused. "I do wonder sometimes if she . . . if there was somebody else."

"You mean, another man?"

"I have nothing at all to rest that suspicion on, except—"

"What?"

Tom sat back. "There was one night, years ago, I got a call from her telling me she had to go to London right then. I mean, that night. I told her it was impossible from Bryher, but she begged me to help. I did. I found a plane, a pilot. She told me no more but I figured it was someone she needed to help. It must have been, well, crucial, an emergency. Daisy was like that, though. She'd go to any lengths to help someone. So problem-solver, yes, she was."

Jury smiled. "A fixer. If there's a good spin you can put on that word." He recalled Josephine Bewley's remark "not until the man sat down" at Flora Flood's table. Jury had wondered at the time who the man had been who had not come to see Flora Flood.

He thought for a moment and then asked, "What is it you miss most about the job, Tom?" For there was no doubt in Jury's mind that he did miss it.

"The applause." Tom smiled and drank off his drink.

Jury thought he must have misheard. But apparently not, for Tom continued.

"The acclaim, the acknowledgment, the interviews, picture in the papers, articles about my cases, the way the rank-and-file cops looked at me, at times almost reverently—the praise, the fame, the standing ovation after a talk I gave. As I said, the applause."

Jury was literally thunderstruck. "*You*, Tom? Come *on*!"

"You believe all of that stuff you used to read in the papers or that book about me and my modesty, my self-denigration, my humility, my dislike of publicity? Sorry to disillusion you. I loved it. I think Daisy was the only one who got it. When I balked at doing the book tour, when I said I wanted to avoid all of the admiration. 'Oh, come on, Dad, drop the pretense. This is me you're talking to. I know you love it.'"

Jury took a long drink and slid down in his chair. "And I bet you didn't."

Tom looked astonished. "I beg your pardon?"

"The pretense was a pretense. My guess is that for some reason you wanted to believe you were that shallow. But I've seen you around other people, listening to them. Your focus is immense. You almost become the other person. I've seen it. The person you're trying to describe is utterly self-involved and that's simply not you."

"You asked what I missed about the job. And that's it." But his tone had changed. "The vanished fame, the lost acclaim, the old success."

"You feel a terrible loss and all that's part of it, but it's the part easiest to talk about. No, what you lost is far more than that. The old success was Daisy."

Tom looked at the fire. In the reflected light, his face looked like a mask of ice. Visible lines, cracking.

"And she's gone, gone, gone. I'm sorry, Tom."

PART II
Fixer

19

The next morning, Jury took the North Circular Road to the Golders Green exit and had only to drive a short distance before he came to a jumble of warehouses and lockups, where he saw CRENSHAW'S CARS and, beneath the name of the business, ALEX CRENSHAW, PROP.

It told him something about Alex Crenshaw: the brevity, the exactness, the lack of flourish. Jury already liked the guy.

Liked him even more when he got out of his car and looked around the lot. If the Porsche next to which he parked his police-issue Cortina was proof of what Crenshaw could do with a fix-up, he was in the right business. The sleek black body looked as if it had never been on the road, let alone had any dents or rust. Jury thought surely it must be a new car until he saw a for sale sign discreetly placed beneath a windscreen wiper. The asking price told him it was definitely not new. And nor could Jury afford this used version. There were a dozen other cars—all

European—out here and all in the same pristine, new-looking condition. But what really won Jury over was the repair shop itself. On the far left was a lighted room, small, and clearly the office. The rest of it consisted of two bays. Above the first hung a sign: CRITICAL CARE. And above the second: ON THE MEND.

Jury smiled. Here was a man who could look at cars not as things just to be pushed and pried and hammered on but as objects with feelings.

The cars out here were definitely out of the critical-care unit: the two Ferraris, the Lamborghini, the Aston Martin, the gorgeous red BMW convertible—all looked mended to within an inch of their lives. It was the BMW Jury was inspecting when he heard a voice at his elbow, a North London accent delivered in a mellifluous voice.

"Good car, that. Engine like a hummingbird. You like it?"

"How could one not?" Jury turned to see a middle-aged man, mildly handsome with a welcoming expression.

"I could give you a great deal on it, if you're interested."

"Mr. Crenshaw, even a great deal would have my bank account running for cover. But if I had money, believe me, you'd have my business. And I know of at least two people who do have money and whose business you're going to get. No, three people, although one of them might be too lazy to drive here from Northamptonshire."

Alex Crenshaw laughed. "Can't say I blame him."

"Her. I'm mightily impressed," Jury added, looking around the lot at cars and bays.

"Thanks. But who do I have the pleasure of impressing? Alex Crenshaw." He held out his hand.

Jury shook it, and with the other hand took out his warrant card. "Richard Jury, New Scotland Yard CID."

"My God. What have you done?" Crenshaw addressed the BMW.

"Nothing to be charged with."

"That's a relief. I just finished fixing this guy up." He patted the car. "Okay, then what have *I* done?"

"Ditto. I'm just after a bit of information."

"Really? Let's go into the office."

Inside was a little overflowing, with a few chairs on which were files and other bunches of paper, a large desk, a half-dozen filing cabinets.

"This is something you've already spoken to police about, recently. A detective chief inspector—"

"Brierly. Northampton police. Just a couple of days ago."

Jury was surprised he recalled these details, and then wondered why he was surprised, given the meticulous care Crenshaw took with his cars. "Right. A few years ago you sold a car to a man named Servino."

"Alfa Romeo. Nice guy. Had his wife with him."

From Crenshaw's expression, Jury surmised she was, possibly, not a "nice girl." "DCI Brierly thought I should talk to you, get more information." Jury knew that Brierly was wrong about the "vague" part; whatever Crenshaw had told him wouldn't be vague, simply not detailed enough. "The thing is, they had an accident some years back and we're just trying to sort it out. And you called police, so I'm thinking there's something here worth pursuing. Why'd you call? And so long after it happened?"

"Understandable. When it happened I was out of the country. When I got back, I found a month-old newspaper in which that accident was reported. Odd that it would be, unless there was something about the Servinos that was newsworthy. Anyway, it was clear that Mr. Servino really liked that Alfa Romeo. It's just that there were a lot of questions. Like, what would happen to the car in a collision? How would it stand up to, say, going up against an embankment or colliding with anything else? The engine's in the rear. Would the driver or the passenger be in more danger? What else could go wrong with an Alfa Romeo? Like braking or things coming loose?

"'Not this Alfa,' I said. 'Things coming loose?' For God's sake. 'Not unless you just loosened things yourself,' I said. 'Take out your lug wrench and—'" He moved his hand and arm in a turn, as if adjusting something. "'Loosen up the lugs and I wouldn't be surprised if a wheel went a little wild when you hit that embankment.' I just laughed."

"So did he ask more questions then?"

"Not him. Her. All he was doing was going around kicking tires. Don't you love the way guys do that? As if it really told him anything about the car." He made it sound like a playground prank.

"*She* was the one concerned about an accident?"

"Yeah, which is what I thought later was peculiar. There was an accident, but she was the one that bought it—I mean, got hurt." He paused. "You know, I almost didn't sell it to them."

"The Alfa? Why not?"

"Thing is, I thought if something goes wrong with my car, I'm afraid they wouldn't bring it back to me for fixing. They'd take it to some cowboy repair guy closer to them. If you see what I mean."

My car. Jury saw. He rose. "Alex, it's been a real pleasure talking to a man who knows what he's doing, who's in the right line. If you think of anything else, let me know." Jury handed over one of his cards. "And as I said, I'm sending business your way."

Alex laughed. "Except for the lazy girl."

"Maybe even her. Good-bye."

20

J ury stood outside of the heavy glass door bearing the name RICE INVESTMENTS for a few very long moments wondering if he should go in. The thought of Vernon Rice kneeling by the body of Nell Ryder that day on the stud farm kept Jury's feet pretty much rooted to the spot.

Was it fair to land Vernon in an emotional quandary in order to get something out of Sydney Cooke, who might not even have something to get? To involve Vernon went against his better judgement.

He went against it and pushed open the door.

Here in the outer office sat Vernon's pretty assistant, going over some papers. It was a small firm that did a large business. It was also very informal. When Jury said he just wanted a few words with Mr. Rice, the assistant smiled, leaned over her desk and looked towards the half open door of her boss.

Jury could see Vernon Rice studying the screens of several monitors, back to the door, hands shoved in pants pockets.

"Go on in, Mr. Jury; he's just daydreaming."

Jury knew Rice wasn't daydreaming, but he went to stand in the doorway. Silently at first, then saying, "Vernon. I need your help."

Vernon Rice turned quickly around, looking first astonished and then pleased. "Richard Jury. You've got it. Come on in."

Jury relaxed and took one of the Italian designer chairs near a coffee table on which rested a pewter pot, steam coming out of the neck, cups and saucers beside it, cream and sugar.

"You're expecting somebody?"

"Yes, you. Have a cup? Rosie always puts out extra cups."

"Good for her. No cream, one sugar. Thanks."

They sat back with their coffees. "Tell me what's going on," said Vernon.

Jury started the story of Tom Brownell and Bryher just as it had started for him and barely stopped to drink or draw breath before Vernon knew as much as he did about Sydney Cooke.

Vernon then rested his head back against his chair and silently warmed his hands on his cup, sipping occasionally from it.

Jury finally broke the silence by saying, "Look, sorry, Vernon, I don't know what I thought you could—"

"Sure you do. You think I can get this something about her mother out of her—this secret. The question is, though, what secret?"

"Her mother—"

"We're assuming it's to do with her mother's death, but why not one of the others? Or something else entirely." He fell silent again and then said, "Shergar."

Jury looked puzzled.

"That great Irish race horse. The one that was kidnapped, possibly by the IRA, and never heard from again." Another silence. Then Vernon said, "When do you want to go?"

"How about now? But I'm barging into your day."

"Oh, go ahead and barge. I'm only doing money. Can we take my car? It's probably faster than yours."

"Anything's faster than mine."

21

In Vernon's Ferrari it took them less than two hours to drive to Ardry End from London.

Vernon was talking about Aggrieved as they pulled up before the columned steps of the house. "Wonderful horse." They were halfway up the wide marble stairs when that very horse came around from the side of the house, Sydney in the saddle.

Vernon Rice stopped cold and stared.

For one heartbreaking moment, Jury thought he was turning away to go back to the car. But then Jury knew Vernon would never turn away. He had looked away for only the moment it would take to master his emotions.

Had she met him at the door in the usual way, Jury knew she would still have reminded Vernon of Nell Ryder, for she had the same coloring, although not as ethereal, and the same build, although not as fragile. But up on a horse, Sydney Cooke would *become* Nell Ryder for Vernon Rice. There'd have been no escaping it. Even though she did not sit that horse as if she were born to it, the pose was identical, and it was the last view Vernon had ever had of Nell.

But what he said to her was, "Remember a horse named Misty Mountain?"

"You must mean Misty Morning," she answered.

"Oh, right."

Jury knew the mistake was deliberate, giving Sydney the tiny victory of correcting him.

"Remember she was ridden by a female jockey?"

"I do," said Sydney.

"You and that horse are the spitting image."

Sydney was out of the saddle and on her feet in front of Vernon in two seconds, immeasurably pleased. It was the first bright smile Jury had seen.

"They didn't win," she added.

"Lost by a hair. Three strides."

"Four."

"Nope. Three."

"I'm sure I'm right."

"I'm sure you're not. I'm Vernon Rice."

Her smile only grew brighter. She liked this little argument. She put out her hand. "Mr. Rice, I'm delighted to meet you. Come on in the house."

In the middle of this sunniness, Melrose Plant came to the door. "Vernon Rice! How are you?"

"Hello, Lord Ardry."

"Don't start that. Melrose will do."

"Then, hello, Melrose."

"See you've met my horse."

"I already knew your horse. But not its rider."

"Keeper, more. Aggrieved has been a bit sick. Stable cough."

"I'm glad he has a stable. When you led him away, I wondered what fate had in store for him."

"Very funny. He's got a goat, too."

"A goat, a girl. Lucky horse."

Sydney's eyes, Jury saw, seemed to be swimming a little, if water could spark.

As they entered the library, Ruthven appeared with two decanters. "M'lord: Talisker or this Lagavulin—" Ruthven turned the bottle to look at the label. "Sixteen-year-old?"

"Wow!" said Vernon. "That's old enough. I'll have a slug of it."

"Let's slug away," said Melrose. "Sit down."

Jury took his usual chair near Melrose's wingback. Vernon sat on the sofa near the fire, and Sydney, without hesitating, sat down beside him.

Ruthven took orders, poured, and said to Melrose, "If it's not a bother, m'lord, Martha would like to see you about the dinner."

"No, of course." Melrose followed Ruthven to the kitchen.

"Do you recall her name?" Vernon asked Sydney.

Sydney looked bewildered. "Whose?"

"The female jockey."

"Oh. Melissa—Herfeld, I think."

"Only female jockey I ever saw."

"Only one there."

"Do you want to be one?"

"Me? God, no. I'm not really in favor of horse racing."

"For not favoring it, you seem to know a lot about it."

"I think it might be inhumane."

"Really? You mean the training the horses go through? But all training is rigorous: baseball, soccer, tennis. It doesn't have to be cruel. I've never known a trainer to mistreat his horses."

"Is that what you do, Vernon? I mean, is your business to do with horses?"

Vernon laughed. "No, except as far as investing is concerned. I have an investment firm in the City. But my stepfather owns a stud farm. I spend a lot of time there. It's where Mr. Plant got Aggrieved. He's a great horse."

Melrose was back in the room, saying, "Macalvie called." He handed Jury a note. "He asked me why the hell you aren't in Exeter. Tom's there."

"He always wants to know why I'm not in Exeter. He's probably holding Tom prisoner."

"But this one is your case too, isn't it?"

"Only by accident."

Vernon said, "What *is* the case, Superintendent? Or should I not ask?"

Given Jury had told him at least that part of it involving Sydney, he didn't blame him for asking, but said, "Another piece of the puzzle. Forgive me if I can't tell you the whole of it. It's an ongoing investigation." To Melrose he said, "Isn't it enough that Brownell's there? Why would he need me?"

Melrose shrugged. "How would I know?"

"That's my grandfather," said Sydney. "That case will get solved, never fear."

Melrose and Jury exchanged a surprised glance. It was the first time they'd heard Sydney mention him, much less compliment him.

"Your grandfather?" said Vernon.

"Thomas Brownell. One of the Metropolitan police's greatest detectives." Sydney looked at the window where Mr. Blodgett was leading Aggrieved back to the barn.

"I've heard of him. It's *Sir* Thomas, isn't it?"

"Yes," said Sydney, still gazing at the window and looking as if she thought titles should be conferred on horses, not humans.

"Then I expect I'd better call him," said Jury, rising.

"Of course," said Melrose. "But Ruthven can bring the phone in here."

"No, no. I'll call from the living room."

"Macalvie," said Jury, as soon as he himself was out of earshot. "What's going on?"

"If you were here, you'd know."

"Well, I'm not, so I don't."

"Moira Quinn. She worked with an agency when she lived in London. Battersea. She . . ." Macalvie's voice trailed off, or, rather, was directed not at the phone but at one of his team with whom he was obviously annoyed. "No, for Lord's sake. Where in hell's Gilly Thwaite? Get her in here, will you?"

Then back to Jury. "Moira got jobs through this agency—Malraux Agency, high-class agency that handles basically French workers and only the best housekeepers, maids, cooks, cleaners—back when you could get people through agencies. When housecleaning meant something."

"It's never meant anything to me."

"Back when *staff* meant something."

"Ditto. Except for Melrose Plant's."

"The good old days—"

"How would you know? You've always lived in a rented flat, same as me."

"Could we get off the class system, Jury?"

"You're the one who was on it. Go ahead with Moira's agency work."

"It's the same one Manon Vinet was listed with. Not surprising, I suppose, as they both ended up at Summerplace."

"So what about Flora Flood's uncle? We've seen sod all of him. He seemed strangely absent from a niece who could be in a hell of a lot of trouble." When Macalvie said nothing, Jury went on: "I expect I should talk to Frank Flood and Lady Summerston."

"At least."

"Do you mean there are others I should talk to? Or that's the least I can do for you?"

"Probably both. I leave that to you. 'Bye."

"Hold on a minute. About Daisy Brownell: from what I've heard, she certainly didn't sound suicidal."

Macalvie was silent for a few moments. Then he said, "Let me tell you about Daisy Brownell. I had a friend. 'Had' because she's dead now. Died when she was in her early forties from some kind of aggressive cancer. Lived in Penzance. She had a twenty-year-old daughter who'd been in an automobile accident and was in hospital in a coma. The accident happened when the girl was nineteen and she'd been in a coma for ten months. No hope, obviously, of coming out of it. They lived on St. Mary's. Her mother, my friend, Annie, went to the hospital in Penzance every day, *every* day and talked to her and read books to her. For ten damned months. Until she died. Annie died, I mean–the mother. From the cancer. But a couple of weeks before she died, I was telling Daisy Brownell this story. Daisy was appalled by the sadness of it. She asked me, the next day, if she could go and see Annie. Was she too sick to have visitors? I said no, but why? I mean Daisy didn't know her, after all. Daisy said she just wanted to talk to her about something.

"And here's the 'something.' Daisy thought Annie would have the terrible burden not only of her own death, but of her daughter's abandonment because Annie wouldn't be able to go to the hospital ever again. Her girl would be left alone. So Daisy said not to worry, she'd go in Annie's place. Annie told me before she died she couldn't believe that a perfect stranger would do this for a person. That doctors told her her daughter, after all, was unreachable and that, of course, it made no difference whether she, Annie, was in the hospital room with her or not. Daisy told her not to believe that, that her daughter was alive and therefore reachable and if she could be reached, Daisy would try to do it.

"So, every day, *every day, Jury*, for the next three months, Daisy Brownell got on a Skybus or the ferry and went to Penzance and talked to and read to Annie's girl. To me, that's mind-boggling. Did this until, finally, the poor girl died. Now, does that sound like a woman who'd kill herself?"

"No, I guess not."

"When Daisy died, I didn't go into headquarters for three days. Just couldn't do it."

That was certainly testament to something.

"If Daisy Brownell has your back, you don't need anything else. She'd do anything for you."

Jury noticed he was using the present tense.

And then Macalvie rang off.

22

The room, like the rest of the house, was narrow and uncluttered, its furniture strategically placed. Chairs sat on either side of the electric fireplace, each with its own little table holding, now, a drink for each guest and a coffee table sat between them. On it sat a stack of magazines and on the magazines a box of chocolates. Jury leaned toward it. *Rive Gauche.*

"I expect I must seem rather indifferent to Flora, I mean, not being there for her."

But Frank Flood gave no reason as to why he hadn't been there.

"No. At least, it's not my job to gauge indifference. But I am curious as to where she manages to get the money to retain such a legal team as she has. There's no better firm than Treadwell's in all of London."

"Oh, that'd be Eleanor paying for that. Flora was like a daughter to them. I expect that's why I've not, you know, always been there myself."

"Police were baffled about motive until they learned that Flora's accident happened when her husband was driving. The car crashed into an embankment."

"It was no accident."

"That's what DCI Brierly told me. But why would her husband have tried to kill her? And in such a way that he could have been killed or at least seriously injured himself?"

"Something she knew about him or at least whoever he was working for."

"You think Flora knew something? From what I understand about Tony Servino, I think it very hard to know anything he couldn't take care of without resorting to engineering a car accident."

"What if it wasn't all that clear? I mean, what if it was something she didn't know she knew, wasn't aware she knew, but which could come out later?"

Jury laughed slightly. "Mr. Flood, you're getting further and further from the obvious explanation: a genuine accident. You really want this to be about Servino."

"But it is, isn't it?"

"Not really. It's about motive: Did Flora really have a motive to shoot him? She was the one with the gun, remember. Not he. And the gun was one of yours."

"There was motive, all right. He was very abusive."

"That would have to be an awful lot of abuse to warrant someone using a gun. Anyway, he didn't need to be."

"What do you mean?"

"It seems to me that Servino depended on his wits. How many times did you actually see him mistreating Flora?"

Frank Flood thought for an unproductive minute. "The thing is, you know what addicts, what alcoholics are like." Frank turned his glass around in his hands.

Since he was now into his third whisky, Jury wondered if this was projection at work. "Actually, I don't. It's too complex."

"Generally speaking."

"That's what I mean: there is no 'general' when it comes to addiction, although AA has to work with that concept or nobody would join."

"Why do you defend him?"

"Because I want to know why you accuse him."

"I'm not the only one," said Frank. "There's Eleanor Summerston for another."

Jury wanted to laugh. *There's half London for the other.* "But there's also Gerald Summerston, from what I've heard. He liked Tony Servino."

"Oh, Gerald." Flood shrugged the man away.

"Why so dismissive?"

"Gerald Summerston liked people who broke things."

"A good metaphor, if I understood how it applied to Summerston. To hear his wife talk, he was anything but an iconoclast."

"Did Eleanor really know him?"

The question was rhetorical, since he was not really asking Jury.

Flood went on. "She certainly seemed not to know how much of an eye he had for other women." He glanced at Jury.

"Was it common knowledge, then?"

"No, not at all. But I think sex was an obsession with him." Frank looked at the box. "As chocolate is for me."

Jury raised the box a little, set it down.

"Ah, yes. Manon's. Only for Gerald, it wasn't the chocolates; it was the chocolatier."

Jury was surprised. "You're talking about the woman found on Bryher?"

"Yes, of course. She had a shop in Paris, that shop." He nodded toward the box. " I've been wondering why she came back here, now."

"Did you know her at all, Mr. Flood?"

Frank shook his head. "Only by way of what Gerald told me, and that not much. Except it was evident he was obsessed with her."

"Enough to leave his wife?"

"Oh, yes. But I don't think he would have. He wouldn't have thought he'd have to."

Jury raised his eyebrows in question.

"Gerald thought he could keep everything going at once." Here he made a gesture of tossing, each hand going up and down, as if throwing plates in the air. He smiled. "The kind of man who was not about to give up something he didn't absolutely have to. Not women, not money."

"But he had both."

Frank Flood smiled. "As I said."

On that ambiguous note, Jury left.

23

But had Frank Flood told that to the Devon-Cornwall constabulary? "No," Frank had said, "it honestly didn't occur to me."

Jury reflected on this possible affair as he drove toward Belgravia and the Summerston house.

What had Manon Vinet been doing in the UK and on Bryher?

It was a variation of this question he asked Lady Summerston after Crick had ushered her into the too-elaborately done drawing room— too much silk and sheer stuff at high windows, too much flounce and flourish on low ottomans and pillows, too much of everything except when it came to Lady Summerston herself, who kept to fine linen and lightweight wool. She was underdone and elegant.

Wearing a spruce-green linen suit, Lady Summerston was handing out cups of tea and talking about her late husband. Had been for the last ten minutes over their first cups, talking about his everlasting consideration for the men under him in Korea, and his heroic action in the saving of them ("You know, of course, about his Conspicuous Gallantry award"); and about his helping two of the servants' children into Oxbridge, one for each school; and about his establishing a foundling hospital in North London.

That was news to Jury. "Foundling hospital?"

"A little place he bought and funded for infants and small children who had been abandoned or were otherwise alone. Gerald was extraordinarily kind," she said. "It's called the Summerston Foundling Hospital. In Bayswater. We read this op-ed piece in the *Times* several years before he died about these abandoned children Social Services found in a house in North London, alone, their parents seeming to have walked out and left them. It was truly pathetic, the state of these children." She paused and put her hand to her head as if thinking about these children's misery, and then went on. "Gerald staffed it with very capable people: two doctors, several nurses, matron and so forth. He went to great lengths. He was really the soul of kindness. It's still there, still operating; a cousin of his took it over."

"Bayswater?"

"Yes. It's on Bayswater Road."

Jury had taken out his notebook and made a note of this, and then said, "I was wondering, Lady Summerston, about your husband's relationship with Flora's husband—the man shot at Watermeadows."

She looked perplexed, or tried to, Jury thought.

He said, "Frank Flood hinted that you didn't like Servino, but that your husband did."

She waved her hand over the tea service, as if waving away Frank Flood. "I have no idea what he's talking about, except that of course Flora and her husband had dinner here a few times."

Jury smiled slightly. "Well, I expect that's something of what Frank Flood is talking about." In addition to the elaborate tea service, on the table sat a box of chocolates, the same brand of chocolates he'd seen at Flood's. He commented on this. "Both you and Mr. Flood like the same chocolates."

"Oh, those. Actually, it was one of my late husband's few indulgences. He loved these chocolates; he found them in Paris and started a sort of running account. They come every so often. I still get them and give some to Frank." She poured the tea.

"From Paris? That reminds me: when your husband was ill, you used this Malraux Agency that handles, almost exclusively, French servants or at least applicants who are very experienced, have served for long periods of time in one or more posts and come highly recommended. Of course, given the agency's fees, I expect that anyone they send out is both experienced and highly recommended."

"You seem to have researched the Malraux Agency rather thoroughly." Her smile was a bit sour.

Jury matched it. "As I should."

"She was just a nurse, Mr. Jury."

"She was just murdered, Lady Summerston."

Eleanor Summerston's response missed being a brief laugh. "Yes. I'm sorry. So I expect you'd want to know as much as possible about her."

"I would. One thing I wonder about is why you chose an employment firm that handles French staff almost exclusively."

"It's because of my late husband's experience in hospital. He'd been wounded in the war and was for some reason deployed to a hospital in Paris. He had several different nurses dancing attendance on him, I imagine."

Her eyes and voice sparkled as she imagined. "Gerald was very attractive to women. As a matter of fact I had to get rid of two different maids because they were showing entirely too much interest in him."

"And did he encourage the interest?"

Jury expected a flat *No!* so was surprised when she said, "Well, I will admit that Gerald loved women. I don't think he could help himself but to flirt a little. Like any man. After all."

Not "any man," thought Jury. A lot of men could avoid a flirtation with a housemaid. After all.

"To answer your question about the agency, the nurse Gerald particularly liked at the hospital in Paris was from the south of France. Aix-en-Provence? Gerald said she was especially good."

"In what way?"

"Attentive without being cloying; smart without being showy; elegant even in her nurse's uniform. Gerald especially like elegance in a woman." Lady Summerston sat up even straighter. "He asked her if her training had included some of these attributes—you know, the kind of attention, not plumping pillows every time she was in the room, for instance. She told him yes, it had. So when it came to hiring a nurse, he asked me to interview ones from this agency."

Jury thought this account so elaborate and contrived it was probably a lie. Why that vast detail to justify using a certain agency?

But he shifted the subject back to Servino.

"Did Gerald have any business dealings with Servino?"

"You keep wanting to tie my husband to Flora's husband. Why?"

"They're already tied, Lady Summerston, given the way that Servino visited him."

"I don't know what you mean."

Yes, she did. He could tell in the way she quickly picked up her cup and just as quickly drank. Lady Summerston was not ordinarily a person who made hasty movements.

"My husband led an exemplary life. And he was the very soul of kindness," she said again.

Soul of kindness he might have been. But exemplary lives did not require a defense, as in that statement she had just made.

What had gone down in Paris? Jury wondered.

"This nurse in the Paris hospital. Did your husband come to know her?"

"What do you mean?"

Given the way her eyes shifted to the silver pot, which she only just then seemed to contemplate raising again, Jury guessed that she knew very well what he meant.

"Only that she seemed to have impressed him enough that he might have seen her again, outside of the hospital."

"I hardly think so, or I expect Gerald would have mentioned it." Pot forgotten, replaced.

Jury tried it on again. "What I was really thinking is that she herself might have tried to see *him*. You said they were all probably dancing attendance on your husband. He didn't even need to try—"

That was a little better. "Of course, that's possible. But again, he would have mentioned it."

"If Gerald mentioned every woman who was attracted to him, you'd have been talking about hardly anything else, I expect." Jury tried a winning smile.

It won. "How true." She laughed.

"Going back to your niece, though—" Had they been there before?

She was relieved to do this. "Ah, yes. Poor Flora. But of course she didn't kill him, Mr. Jury. You can be sure of that."

"I'd like to be, Lady Summerston, but as we were saying at Water-meadows, it's difficult."

"Tony Servino was not a nice man. I can't understand how my husband put up with him."

"He liked him, though."

She both shook and nodded her head, a difficult denial of the truth for her. "It's true that Gerald invited him here. Said after all he was Flora's husband. A few times, he even brought a friend with him."

"What friend?"

"Oh, someone Gerald thought entertaining."

Jury didn't prompt her.

"What was his name?" Her fist gently hit her forehead as if the mind could take the beating. "Scruffy little man . . . another Italian."

Jury smiled. Scruffiness foretold. "Another besides Tony Servino, you mean? But he was English, Lady Summerston."

"Not *truly* English, Superintendent, though. Italian heritage, certainly." She returned to the friend's identity. "Vincent—They called him 'Vince'. . . Morini? No, Mori. That was it: Vincent Mori. As I said, Tony occasionally brought him here to dinner. For some reason, Gerald took to him. But Gerald was quite egalitarian."

Jury put the egalitarianism down to the Gerald-myth. "Would you happen to know where he lives?"

She raised an eyebrow. "No, I don't. I seem to recall references to Limehouse. Yes, I think that was where he lived."

"You really didn't like him, did you?"

"This Mori person? Of course not—"

"No. I mean Tony Servino."

"No, I didn't. I've said before that he was a real scoundrel. He had other women. He cheated people, including his partner, as I recall. And he victimized Flora both physically and verbally. He certainly wasn't worthy of her."

"How would you assess Flora's worthiness?"

Eleanor frowned. "What do you mean?"

"Just that. What has your niece done or been that would raise her so far above her husband?"

"Breeding, for one thing. Her father was a respected barrister. Tony's father owned a fish and chips shop."

"Well, that would certainly earn him my sergeant's respect."

"I beg your pardon?"

"Sorry. What else about Flora?"

"She's highly educated: Oxford."

"And her husband lacked education?"

She sighed with impatience. "Mr. Jury, I've told you about Tony Servino, how he victimized her."

"Yes, you have; only in this case, the victim was Tony." Jury took a last, cold sip of tea and rose. "Thank you for your time, Lady Summerston."

At the bottom of the steps, he pulled out his phone. "Wiggins, there's someone I want you to find. Get his address, if possible: Vincent Mori. He might have lived at one time in Limehouse."

"Who is this, boss?"

"Good friend of Tony Servino. And possibly partner."

"One he ripped off?"

"To hear Lady Summerston tell it, Tony ripped off everybody. A 'real scoundrel,' she said. Still, Gerald Summerston seemed to like him."

"Maybe they were scoundrels together."

Jury liked that. "The virtuous Gerald Summerston?"

"Sounds a little too virtuous for my tastes."

"I'll wait in the car. Call me back when you have something."

"Knightsbridge, not Limehouse," said Wiggins. "Moved up a bit, looks like." He gave Jury an address.

"That's not far. Just around the corner. Thanks, Wiggins."

No one answered the bell in the little house in the Brompton Road, but as Jury turned away, a man who'd come out of the house next door said, "You looking for Vince?"

"I am, yes."

"Try the Grapes. He's usually over there around this time. You know, it's just down the road." He nodded his head to the right.

Jury thanked him and returned to his car.

24

Jury had drunk in the Bunch of Grapes a number of times; since the last time there had been some refurbishment. Unnecessary refurbishment. Some things are best left alone.

A lot of smoke from a lot of cigarettes obscured faces. He figured Mori would be one for standing at the bar. Jury looked down its length as he pulled out his phone and found the picture Wiggins had sent. A slightly pudgy face topped by curly dark-brown hair. The face was sitting or standing at the end of the bar and Jury made his way to it.

"Are you Mr. Mori?"

Vincent Mori looked over his shoulder. "Who?"

Jury had his warrant card out and held it up to Mori's eyes.

"I didn't do it," said Vincent Mori and returned to his pint.

"Nobody says you did."

"Well, good. So what is it?"

Jury signaled the barman for two drinks.

"The Met is buying these days?"

"Yep."

"If I didn't do it, why are you here?"

"Somehow I get the impression maybe you did."

"Don't push your luck—oh, Christ. How could I be so dumb? It's about Tony, isn't it?"

"It's about Tony."

Mori lowered his head and half-framed it with one of his hands. "Bloody hell."

It was the first sign of emotion Jury had seen, and it looked like strong emotion. "I'm sorry, Mr. Mori."

"Yeah. Me too. Tony was supposed to be invincible. But why would his goddamned wife shoot him?"

"Self-defense."

"Ridiculous. Tony didn't do guns, didn't beat up women. Never."

"Apparently, he got to the house in a rage."

Mori snorted a laugh. "Tony didn't do rages, either. If she shot him, she meant to shoot him going in."

"Why?"

Vincent shrugged. "You think I know?"

"Probably . . ."

Mori only looked at him.

"What I'm here for is your opinion, your ideas about Tony Servino. You're the only person I know so far who's defending him, who thinks pretty highly of him."

Vincent laughed again. "I can believe that."

"What I've heard about Servino is that he was a womanizing alcoholic, a man who would sell out anybody, including his partners—of which you're one—a gambler who cheated all the time, a rotter, a scoundrel, a man who very possibly tried to kill his wife by means of a car accident."

Mori started laughing softly halfway through this description, and by the time Jury got to the attempt on Flora's life, he was laughing so hard people were staring.

"What's so funny, Mr. Mori?"

In the middle of a choked laugh, Mori said, "Sorry, what was your name?"

"Richard Jury. CID superintendent."

"Mr. Jury, people just didn't get it. I don't deny a lot of your description—he drank, he gambled—but won. What I do deny is the out-of-control implication. Tony was never out of control. He had control of everything he did. Tony was a fixer. You didn't get that? A fixer."

Jury frowned. "What?"

"You want an example? Buy me another drink and I'll tell you." As if he were literally waiting for the fresh drink before he gave out any information, Vincent leaned against the bar, arms out, hands folded. When the drinks came, he turned back to Jury. "You remember that Cholmondeley thing several years back. A decade back. Never ended up coming out. This British peer, Earl of I think Harwood, the younger brother of the Marquess of Cholmondeley, got caught in a call box out on an A road near a Little Chef. He was in the box with a young guy named Billie Whitelaw—

"Going at it. Someone took a picture, Harwood was still holding the telephone receiver." Vincent laughed. Then he went on. "You imagine how Cholmondeley would have liked the family name dragged through the press and the courts if it came to that. He gets his bank of solicitors on it. They try to buy off Billie Whitelaw, but Billie refuses to be bought. My guess is he likes the publicity, likes the idea of a trial because he pretty much holds the winning hand. So the legals get Tony Servino to buy the kid off. No way.

"Tony finds out everything he can about Billie, looking for arrests, citations, anything he can use. Kid is clean as a whistle. Nothing. Nil. But in the course of looking at Billie's life—what he hated, what he loved—Tony sees what he wanted was Africa. Apparently the kid's dream is to be a safari guide. Safari guide, for God's sake. Tony searches out the businesses that use them—the luxury camps, the ones in the bush and so forth. He looks for the ones less solvent, those in financial trouble. He finds a tented camp, a really pricey one in Kenya on the edge of bankruptcy, contacts the owner and tells him he can take care of the financial problem if he'll get his guides to take on this kid as an intern. Well, that deal is easy to do; the camp has nothing to lose and a lot to gain.

"Tony goes to Billie Whitelaw and lays this out. His dream will come true if he forgets about the phone booth and the Little Chef and hands over the photo. And the scandal died on its feet."

Jury was fascinated, listened, gave it some thought. "One thing I find strange, is a man like Servino would marry at all, much less marry a woman like Flora Flood."

Vincent shrugged. "I don't know, except it wasn't her money."

"And what about this car accident?"

"What about it?"

"There seems to be a question of whether it was really an accident."

"Look, I think you got the whole relationship backward. She says she wanted out; he didn't. It was the other way around. Tony wanted the divorce. She was crazy about him. Women usually were. I think he loved her, would have kept going except she was so jealous, always questioning, always suspicious. He couldn't stand being watched. Yeah, he had a bit on the side. Sure. But if Tony had wanted in or out of that marriage, he could have done it; he could have walked away. Tony could always walk away. Except—" Vincent stopped, looked down at the bar.

Jury leaned closer. He could have sworn the man was near tears. "Except for what, Vincent?"

"His little kid. Except for when he died. Tony's baby."

"My God, how awful."

"It was awful, all right. I never saw a man so grief-stricken. Never. It was like, five, six years ago. They lived in Mayfair. He went home one night . . ."

25

Six years before

That night, Tony Servino walked through the front door of his Mayfair house and called out to his wife, who didn't answer. He did not stop to wonder where she was, but immediately made for the nursery upstairs and the baby he liked to call "the little guy." Sammy was only ten months old, but they had been the best ten months of Tony Servino's life. Sometimes he thought they'd been the *only* ten months of his life.

He heard Flora on the phone in the parlor as he made his way upstairs and into the room where the crib was, one of the three rooms that comprised the nursery. The one to the left was the bath, where he went next, and where he heard sounds of water splashing, coming from the bathinette. He didn't get this, for the room was both dark and empty.

Or so it seemed. He went to the baby's bath and then knew the splashing sounds were being made by water dripping slowly from the whale-covered faucet into the little blue whale-shaped bath that Sammy could sit up in. But to Tony's horror, Sammy was—*under* the water. The little arms that had been flailing and the legs that had been pushing stopped. In another second, Tony had pulled him out, Tony yelling for help, seeing the crumpled face smooth out into nothing and the mouth that had been trying to take in air and taken in only water close. Tony put the baby facedown on a folded towel, still yelling for help and pushing on Sammy's back, not knowing how to give artificial respiration to a baby.

"Sammy!" Tony screamed.

Sammy couldn't cry.

He yelled for help again, but neither voice nor footstep came rushing up the stairs. Where were they all?

Tony thought ambulance, and then that he could get to the hospital faster in his Alfa Romeo than any ambulance. The hospital was only five minutes and three stoplights away. He wrapped the baby in a blanket, pushed him under his overcoated right arm, ran down and out without shutting the door and jumped into his car, glad he'd left it by the curb and not in the driveway. He streaked off, horning through two red lights, knowing and not-knowing the little guy was dead, weeping all the way to the hospital.

He left the car directly outside the ER, ran inside, gave Sammy over to a nurse, who gave him to a doctor, and stood staring after them down the long, empty corridor.

It was less than two minutes before the doctor came out and towards Tony. The doctor was a kindly looking man, who said in low tones how sorry he was, but that the baby was dead.

Tony clutched at the doctor's arms, then gave up and put his head on his shoulder and wept even more.

"His mother?" The doctor put his arm around the father and asked the only question he could think to ask.

Tony shook his head.

The doctor knew questions were pointless, anyway. Every answer would be a headshake. Nothing to convey.

He could only watch as Tony moved to a place in the waiting room, walking like a young man old.

26

He had sat in the hospital waiting room for a time he couldn't measure, calling no one, doing nothing, staring. Finally, he had driven himself back to the house, trudged up the stair he had rushed down with Sammy, up to the front door and inside to be confronted by all of those faces absent—how long? Thirty, forty minutes ago? An hour? Two?

Suddenly, as if called back from an anywhere Tony couldn't envision, they stood, rigid and heard the news: Sammy was dead.

He did not take off his coat. He would never take it off again in this house. He went to the drinks table and poured himself half a tumbler of whisky and waited. He did not try to make sense of the senseless, or to comprehend the incomprehensible. He did not even ask it aloud—Where were you?

There was first the disbelief, the cobwebby explanations that meant to excuse each of them from guilt, no one admitting she was supposed to have been there, supposed to have stayed in, supposed to have had the charge of Sammy. "It was my night off . . ." "I wasn't told to watch the baby . . ." "Mrs. Servino knew I was going to . . ."

It went on and on, the appropriately horrified responses all tempered by the accusations flying back and forth among these women—nurse, nanny, au pair, mother—none of them claiming one iota of responsibility.

Tony did not even try to follow the drift of the argument. Tony Servino, a master at getting to the bottom of things, would never get to the bottom of this.

Only the old cook, Rebecca, responded in the right way. She rushed to him, weeping his name: "Mister Tony, Mister Tony, Mister—"

He put his arms around her. "It's all right, Reba; it's all right."

And he was gone.

The Mayfair was the first hotel he came to and he pulled up in front and left his car for the valet and went in.

It made no sense to call her because there was no way she could get to him, no way. It was by now midnight.

But he called her anyway.

On the other end of the line she picked up the telephone and heard silence.

She knew him even by his silences. "Tony! Tony, what is it? What's wrong?"

More silence that she didn't break into. She waited.

"Sammy." And then sobbing.

No, she thought. Something's happened to the baby. No. "Tony, sweetheart. What?"

"He's—"

Sick? Dying?

"Dead."

Dear God, no. "Are you at home? Where are you?"

"Not home. The Mayfair."

"Stay." She was already out of her nightdress, into her clothes. "I'll be there."

"There's no way from there. There's no way for you to come tonight."

"I'll be there. I'll come."

She rang another number. "I've got to get to London. Now. Right now."

"What? That's impossible, honey. It's the middle of the night. The ferry's schedule—"

"I don't care about the ferry's schedule. I don't want the ferry. I need a plane."

An even more frenzied "*What?* But one can't land—"

"Something can. Something. Come on. You know there's some stretch, of land or water. Get Enrique."

"He's a stunt pilot, honey. Why? For God's sakes!"

"I need a stunt. You can do anything, Daddy, anything. And please don't waste time asking questions."

"But—"

"Or arguing. If you don't get someone, I will, it'll just take a lot longer. So *please*."

Half an hour later the little seaplane came down on a stretch of moonlit water not far from the sand. She paid a fisherman a huge sum to take her out in his boat to the plane, he saying what she was paying was much too much, and she saying nothing is too much.

She felt she was being blown into the plane more than just heaving herself up and in with the help of the pilot's outstretched arm. The plane took her to the mainland and a small airport and a jet. Thence to London City Airport and a helicopter to London's center and the hotel, where the helicopter hovered above the roof. The pilot yelling over the noise about the rope ladder, not substantial but not too long and that would get her to within a couple of feet of the roof, and for God's sakes to be careful.

She reached over, planted a kiss on his cheek, gave him a smile and a thumbs-up. She twirled more than climbed down the ladder and dropped to where two hotel valets stood, arms up to grab at her. Then running to the roof door, hauling it open, down one flight, then two, three, to the corridor and the door of the room, where she stopped to draw in breath and thank them.

Forgetting to turn on the light, forgetting to lock the door, Tony sat in his room, still thinking about that phone call, knowing that she couldn't come, yet comforted by her promise to come. An impossible promise, but she held it out nonetheless. This kept him from thinking about Sammy for tiny stretches of time—just knowing that someone could feel the loss as he himself felt it. But all the same, he really needed her now, and there was no way she could come. There were footsteps, a little talking outside his door, and he'd started to get up when the door opened. Because his room was in darkness, the light flooded in from the hall, outlining the dark figure standing in his doorway.

"Tony."

"My God. You've come—" His head dropped in tears. "Sammy." He choked.

She fairly flew across the room and flung her arms around his neck. And so she came.

PART III
Soul of
Kindness

27

He went home one night . . .

Jury sat in his flat the next morning with his mug of cold tea thinking about last night's conversation with Vincent Mori in the Grapes. How terrible, to come home and find your baby drowned in its bath and no one there. How could that happen? Flora Flood had said nothing about a child. Vincent had asked him, *"For God's sakes, Tony, why didn't you call?"* He said he had called somebody. Somebody came. *"Who, Vincent?" "I don't know. All Tony said was 'somebody came.'"*

He was a nice guy . . . a bit on the side . . . If Daisy Brownell has your back . . . Fixer.

Jury sat the cold mug on the floor, picked up his land line and called Brian Macalvie.

* * *

When Jury walked into his office at New Scotland Yard an hour later, he found Sergeant Wiggins, not ordinarily a bookish man, hunched over a book that lay on his desk, his mug of tea apparently forgotten. His boss had certainly been, the way Wiggins squinted up at him as if a perfect stranger had barged in.

Jury gave a brief laugh. "What are you reading, Wiggins? Looks like a page-turner."

Wiggins held it up. "It is, sir." *Brownell*. Jury recognized the book Melrose had been reading.

"Ah yes, *our* Tom Brownell."

"Well, yours, not mine. I haven't been working with him. He sounds brilliant."

Jury smiled. "He is. Very smart, certainly. Very modest and unflashy. But getting to this case, what have you learned about the Bryher victim?"

"Madeline—or Manon, which is a kind of nickname—Vinet," said Sergeant Wiggins, "had a lot of different jobs: managed a restaurant once, worked as a nurse or nurse's aide, was a partner in a book shop, Libre Albertin, then worked in a chocolate shop she finally bought in Saint-Germain-des-Prés. Ran that for years with a friend or partner. Commander Macalvie thinks you should go to Paris and talk to this co-owner friend and see what you can find out."

"Commander Macalvie thinks I should go anywhere in the world he himself doesn't want to. Why doesn't he just ring her?"

"He said he tried, but she wasn't very responsive, and, anyway, you're better at that sort of thing. He couldn't get anything out of her."

Jury gave a dismissive laugh. "Better at it than he is? I can't imagine him saying that. Did he say anything about the photo and Matthew Bewley?"

Wiggins screwed up his face. "Maybe that's what I didn't understand. He said he'd ring you later about the ID. What's he talking about?"

"An identification."

Wiggins rolled his eyes. "That's generally what ID means; identifying what?"

"Tell you later. What about Gerald Summerston?"

"He was in Korea, led a regiment, got in between a machine gun and his men. That's what he got the Conspicuous Gallantry Medal for. Ended up wounded in a hospital in Paris. I can get more by searching the War Office Registers, I expect."

"Get me George Martin over at MOD."

Wiggins looked surprised. "You can't stand him, guv. He talks and talks and talks but rarely says anything you want."

"I know. But he's got the information, if he can get round to it. So get him."

The phone rang and Wiggins picked it up, listened. "It's Mr. Plant. Wants to talk to you."

Jury picked up. "Hey, what's going on?"

"I'm on my way to Watermeadows. Flora Flood's really in a bad way—"

"I'd be too, in the circumstances."

"I wish you'd come to Ardry End."

"If you want me to, sure. But not until day after tomorrow. Maybe for breakfast."

"Breakfast's good. Thanks."

Jury rang off, nodded to Wiggins, said, "George Martin?"

Wiggins picked up the phone with a shrug that said "suit yourself" and made the call.

When he was finally routed to Martin, Wiggins nodded to Jury. "George, my God! It's been a long time—"

This standard comment received a rattling reply through a receiver that Jury held away from his ear. When the rattle stopped, or at least abated, Jury said, "Listen, George, I wonder if you can give me something about an army second lieutenant named Gerald Summerston. Korean War. He got a medal for valor or something equally wonderful— No. No . . . Oh, come on, George, I'm not asking you to break open a sealed file . . ." Again, Jury held the phone away, while Wiggins looked at him with a smirk.

"What?" he said, bringing it back to his ear. "Idle curiosity? Now why would I be sitting here, idling with curiosity? No, I haven't read the *Telegraph* in weeks. Suing who for what? Who's Ernie—?" Here Jury signaled for Wiggins to pick up and mimed note-taking.

Reluctantly Wiggins dragged over his notebook.

"How can he sue him? Gerald Summerston's dead." Another rattling answer revved up like a car engine desperately trying to get from zero to ninety in thirty seconds.

Wiggins's hand raced across his notepad as George Martin's race with intelligibility continued. Jury put the receiver down again, raised it every so often and made a sound to let George know he was there before the receiver went down again. And again. Martin was like a man shoveling earth into a grave with lunatic speed as if afraid that corpse or coffin or information would suddenly rise up and announce itself. After two or three minutes of this outpouring, silence fell as did Wiggins's head on his pad.

Jury said, "Thanks so much, George. What? Green Park? Afraid I can't . . . but, surely you've told me everything I need to know . . . You don't want anyone else to hear?. . . Look, George, maybe next week we can get together." As the rattle kept up, Jury kept inching the receiver towards the cradle and making noises of departure: "I've got to go, George. Thanks. Bye." He locked the receiver down. At least he felt he was locking it. Never to be picked up again.

"You got that, Wiggins?" Jury asked.

"Unfortunately, yes. All I have to do is comb through it for highlights and make sense out of them."

"He wanted me to meet him in Green Park so that he could tell me the rest. Sometimes I wish Le Carré had never written *The Spy Who Came in from the Cold.* But well done, Wiggins. You deserve a reward: how about a meal at Ruika?"

Wiggins sat up brightly.

"I got nothing on my end from that call," said Jury, "except there was a bit in some column of the *Telegraph* about a legal suit . . . no, I'm not sure it was legal . . . about Summerston being sued."

"His estate, sir. I'll tell you at Ruika."

Information held hostage while they made their way to a car and the restaurant.

Ruika was Wiggins's favorite place, second only to the Starrdust in Covent Garden. He loved studying a menu from which he always ordered the same thing. He loved bypassing the long line of frustrated customers waiting for tables to empty and who regarded these two interlopers as breaking some ancient law of patronage.

Their tea was brought. They ordered crispy fish and shrimp tempura.

"OK, Wiggins, get out that notebook and tell me if there's anything of interest."

Wiggins's eyes moved back and forth along the pages of his notebook. "Man named Ernest Temple. His father, Luther, was in Korea—this was in '57 or '58—in a platoon led by Summerston. It looks like . . ." Wiggins frowned over the notes. "In the Battle of the Imjin River Summerston went behind lines to take out machine-gunners, saving the lives of his men. It's this the Temple guy is disputing. 'That medal was rightfully me dad's' is what Martin says he said."

Jury set down his tiny tea cup without drinking. "That doesn't sound good."

Wiggins shrugged.

Jury nodded toward the notebook. "There must be something else in there to explain this."

Wiggins shook his head. "Something about challenging the Queen's awards."

"Meaning this Ernest Temple."

Wiggins went on plowing up words.

"Where's George Martin getting this?"

"I think he rang him up, sir. Temple."

Their fish and shrimp were set before them and the little server went off. She was probably Danny Wu's aunt or great-aunt or cousin. The restaurant was definitely family run.

Jury's mobile did its Tweety Bird ringtone and he yanked it out. It was Macalvie.

"Good shot, Jury. For once. Yep. You were right. Both Matthew Bewley *and* what's-her-name—"

"Josephine?"

"Right. Both of them said the fellow in the photo was the one in the Hell Bay Hotel restaurant. This was years ago, though."

"I know."

"He'd sat down at a woman's table, but their impression was that it was pure chance, that he hadn't gone there to see this woman."

"Tony Servino was there to see another one. Yes, years ago," Jury added sadly. Then he said, "Thanks, Macalvie." Jury was about to ring off when he quickly brought the mobile back and said, "What do you mean, 'for once'?"

But Macalvie had already gone.

Jury tapped his phone again, found it juiceless. "Wiggins, can you ring Tom Brownell? This is dead." He held up his phone.

Wiggins tapped a number, listened, then handed it to Jury. "Brownell."

"Tom, it's Richard. Listen. Have you read the *Telegraph* lately?" Jury laughed. "Nor have I. But there was a column in the paper a couple of days ago." Jury summarized Wiggins's summary. "I think you should talk to this Temple."

"In what capacity? I have no Met standing."

"Just do the standard 'I'm not here in any official capacity.'"

"'Official capacity' might be the only way to get him to talk to me."

"Not you, Tom. You can get a response from a man in a coffin. No wonder you had a hundred percent clear-up rate."

"Don't go there."

"Okay. Ninety-nine, then. I was thinking we might want to visit that foundling hospital that Summerston funded."

"Tomorrow morning? Around ten, eleven?"

"That's fine. Tomorrow afternoon I'm going to go to Paris."

"Paris?"

"I want to see Manon Vinet's partner, the woman who's been working there for years. When I come back I'm going to Northants, to Ardry End. I want to talk to Flora Flood. Although, when I think about it, that had better be left to you. She likes you."

"In her position, she shouldn't like anybody."

"You think she's that vulnerable?"

"I think she's that guilty." Tom rang off.

28

The Summerston Foundling Hospital was, strictly speaking, neither for foundlings nor a hospital. It was, however, making gestures in both directions by way of the rubbed bronze figurines that sat on either side of the massive gate, across whose center was positioned a bronze plaque with the single word SUMMERSTON. One figure was a hunched woman wrapped in scarves, face bent over a small child similarly wrapped. The figure on the other side stood much straighter, arms extended, perhaps intending to take what the hunched woman held. This figure was uniformed as, possibly, a nurse.

To open the gate, the plaque with the name on it had to split in two, perhaps suggesting the Sisyphean nature of Summerston's work. Jury had never seen such pretense fashioned as entryway.

*   *   *

The woman who rose from the high-backed chair behind the uncluttered desk was the embodiment of "matron." Tall, stout to her earlobes, dressed in navy blue garnished with unnecessary bits and bobs of gold— brooch and buttons—she wore an expression of recent upheaval that was probably her default look. Her name was Mrs. Maltings, according to the little metal plate on the desk.

As she was saying she'd been told of their coming, a little girl strayed into their presence. She looked cute, curly-haired and human.

"Marcia," said Mrs. Maltings, "you should be having tea at Play-Time." The woman made fluttery "go-away" motions with her fingers.

But Marcia, seeing two new and good-looking men, was not so easily routed. She presented the much-handled cloth horse she was carrying to Tom, saying, "This is Sunny."

"Ah! And do you ride Sunny round the gardens out there?"

Marcia clapped both her hands and Sunny up to her face. What? A grown-up man thinking a girl could ride a toy horse? What a wonderful break in grown-up experience!

Part of which was coming round the desk to spoil it all. She was calling out to an as yet invisible party: "Sandra?"

As if she'd been waiting in the wings, a young woman appeared and hurried over to them.

"Sandra, you really must see better to your charges."

But upon seeing the two men, Sandra seemed no more interested in seeing to things than had Marcia.

Nor was Tom, who crooked his finger at Marcia as he took a packet of gummy bears out of his coat pocket. "If I give you these, will you promise to share them with your friends in playtime? But only if they promise they won't let the gummy bears ride Sunny around?"

Sandra was as happy about the bears as was Marcia, for it gave them a way out without being ordered by Mrs. Maltings.

"For a policeman, you have quite a way with children," she said to Tom.

"I have quite a way with murder suspects, too."

Not knowing quite what to do with this piece of unasked for (and undesired) information, Mrs. Maltings started showing them around. The hospital was small, with perhaps ten patient rooms, a delivery room, a café-like room, a children's playroom populated that afternoon by a half-dozen little ones, a large waiting room. The hospital-sterility was considerably softened by warm, homelike touches, such as small-figured wallpaper in patient rooms, along with good linen and pretty coverlets and blankets on the wider-than-average hospital beds.

"It's a very pleasant look; I'd think those who got admitted here would find it a world apart from what they're used to. Disease, drugs, hunger, want—"

"Indeed. Many of the people who come here are simply malnourished and worn out from living in the streets."

"Or pregnant?"

She nodded. "Those women are free to take their infants with them or to put them up for adoption or foster care. Most choose to do that if they haven't acquired any way to take care of themselves whilst in here."

"It's one woman in particular we're interested in. Manon Vinet, a French woman who might have come here about six years ago."

Mrs. Maltings straightened as if with rigorous intent to protect the hospital's information. "I can't discuss individual patients, Inspector. For that you'd have to speak to the doctor who was in charge at the time."

"Who is—?"

"Was. Dr. Park. Dr. Howe Park."

"So, may I speak to him?"

"Dr. Park has retired. He lives in St. Just."

"In Cornwall?"

"Yes." Her mouth tightened as if even that disclosure made her unhappy.

"Well, can you give me his address? His phone number?"

She seemed doubtful even as to that. "I believe I have that information in my office."

As they walked toward that office, Jury tried to loosen her up by commenting on Summerston's and the designer's superb taste as he looked again at the well-appointed rooms they passed.

Tom said, "Gerald Summerston appears to have thought of everything."

Loosen up she did, almost glowing with approval. "Indeed he did. And so very generously supplied the funds to carry out these thoughts. The kindest person I think I've ever known."

"The soul of it," said Jury.

"Indeed."

29

"You was to take me to the Mucky Duck later," said Carole-anne Palutski on the following day. She was busy adding fake gems to her fingernails. There were tiny bits arranged on Jury's coffee table.

"Sorry. We'll do that when I come back." Jury was stuffing a few items into an overnight bag. "Shouldn't you be at work at the Starrdust?"

"Andrew gave me the afternoon off." She studied the various fake bits on the table.

"Why? So you could enamel your nails?" He tossed in his shaving kit.

She ignored that and went on with her own line: "I don't see why you have to *go* to Paris. You could just ring this person and ask your questions over the phone."

"Because I'd be far more likely to get answers if I'm there in person."

"Why? Because of your looks and charm?"

The furthest thing from Jury's mind. He'd been thinking of human nature. But he went along with Carole-anne. "Of course."

"Well, you don't have them."

"Thanks."

"Or that much of them." She corrected herself and her little fingernail, on which she repositioned some bit of ruby. "So you'd just as well pick up the phone and ask your questions that way." She held out her hand to inspect the installation. "It makes Mrs. W. nervous when you're gone for overnight."

Meaning it made Carole-anne nervous.

Wiggins drove him to Heathrow, where he got the three o'clock flight to Paris.

"It's 4:00 p.m. there; the shop's open until 7:00, so you'll have plenty of time to get there. And this Gabrielle will be there; I checked on that."

"And does Gabrielle have a last name?"

"Belrose."

It was a little shop in a little street in Saint-Germain-des-Prés. A bell made a tinny sort of music when he opened the door.

A woman—looking more like a girl—stood behind one of the three long glass display cases, choosing chocolates to place in small, dark paper cups lining a black-and-gold box with which Jury was now quite familiar.

"Pardon me," said Jury, "but are you Gabrielle Belrose?"

She looked up over the case. "*Oui.*"

"May I speak with you for a few moments, mademoiselle?" When she hesitated, he said, "I'm a policeman—"

"The Sûreté? Again?"

Jury tried to work up a comforting smile. "The British version. New Scotland Yard. Not again. It's about Manon Vinet, the owner. You were a good friend?"

Her eyes rimmed with tears. "*Oui.*"

"I don't want to upset you. I'm sure you've had enough dealings with police, but—"

She looked away. "Enough."

Jury said, "Look, if you'd rather not talk to me, that's all right. I'll just go away."

Her smile at that was slight, her lips pale, as if her face were refusing comfort and color, and her face was very pretty indeed. "I did not know police went away."

"This one does." Jury fished the hotel card from his pocket, wrote his name and mobile phone number on the back and shoved it across the counter. "If you feel like talking to me, I'm at this hotel. Thanks, Gabrielle." Jury turned to leave.

Then she exclaimed, "*Attendez!*"

That, he thought, meant "Wait!" and he turned back.

"I do not mind talking to you. I'm closing the shop up now. Could we perhaps go for a drink?"

"We certainly could. But let's go one better. Let's go for dinner. I passed a nice-looking restaurant, just down the Rue des Beaux-Arts."

"Le Vin d'Or? But that's . . . *trés, trés cher*!"

"Good. It's time Scotland Yard paid for something *trés cher.*"

She looked down at her skirt. "I don't know if I'm dressed—"

"I may not be, but believe me, you're dressed for anything. Close up and let's go."

Whether they were dressed for it could not be discerned from the smile of the maître d' at Le Vin d'Or, who seemed happy to lead them to a table despite their not having a reservation. And the table was well placed against a wall made warm-looking by a smoked-glass sconce directly above it, complemented by a tea candle beneath it that the maître d' lighted.

He placed very small menus before them, not the dinner menus but ones listing appetizers and numerous drinks.

It was up to their waiter to hand over the larger-than-life dinner menus and take their order for drinks. Jury looked around. "This place is spectacular in its very lack of pretense." The staggering prices he thought were justified from sampling the ambience and the friendly service before he'd sampled the food. "Don't even think about it," he said, nodding toward the menu, when he saw her eyes widen. "Just order what you want and dig in."

Her bell-like laugh came again. It was as if she'd brought the candy shop with her.

They both ordered the same thing—fillet of beef and accompanying side dishes, whose names were too difficult for him to bother sorting out so he let her do it.

"How long have you been working at Manon's, Gabrielle?"

"Friends call me Gaby. I started about nine or ten months after she opened it, so it's been about eleven years."

"You probably knew her better than anyone. God knows, better than Scotland Yard, as we didn't know her at all. That's why your help is so important. You understand."

She nodded, sadly, watching the waiter pour their wine.

"That is, we do know she had at one time been involved with Gerald Summerston."

"Yes."

Jury had been pretty sure this trip wasn't a waste of time. Now he was even more sure.

"Did you know him?"

"Yes. He came to the shop often. That's how she met him. He loved chocolate."

"Did you like him?"

"No."

The abruptness of the answer startled him. He said nothing, only waited until she looked up at him.

"He was not a good man." She paused. "He had a wife." She regarded him as if expecting a challenge. "You think perhaps in France we . . . ah . . . blink at such behavior."

"No, I don't think that. What sort of life was he offering her?"

The waiter was setting their plates before them, pouring more wine, softly treading off.

"I feel life was not what he was offering at all. Even though he told her he would divorce his wife and marry her."

"He was lying?"

"*Oui*. But she believed him. This man was very charming. Very. I think he could have convinced her of anything. But he was sexually obsessed. It seemed to be all he thought about; he tried seducing nearly every woman he knew. He even tried it with me. Of course, I didn't tell her. But I have a feeling she knew, anyway." She cut into her fillet. After a few bites, she picked up her wine glass and sat looking at it. "You know, Manon drank a lot. A bottle of wine a day. Every day. Then, a little while after he left Paris, telling her he'd be back in a few weeks, she stopped drinking. Completely stopped. I asked her why and she said, 'Because Gerald thinks I drink too much.'" Gaby frowned.

"An odd time to do it, to stop, after he'd left."

"I thought so. But she had her reasons. And then a little while later, perhaps a month later—and of course, he hadn't come back to Paris—she left."

"She left?"

"To go to London. He contacted her to tell her he was sick. He wanted her to come. He'd made arrangements, he told her, for her to come to the Summerston place as a nurse."

"But Lady Summerston wouldn't—"

"Apparently she would. For some reason she accepted the nurse-charade. Madeline—Manon—told me it had something to do with a private hospital where he had told his wife she worked. I didn't understand any of this, but—"

Jury thought of the foundling hospital, which Summerston himself owned. "And when Gerald died, she returned to Paris?"

"Not for a few months. Two, I think. She spent them in the North at some friend's place." Her puzzlement was evident.

Jury pushed his plate away. "I think she spent them at that private hospital. She was pregnant, don't you think? That's why she stopped drinking a bottle a day. And she was gone long enough—about six months?—to have had his baby, right? I'm guessing she told him she was pregnant and might have given him an ultimatum which, in any event, he couldn't have done much about as he was genuinely and terminally ill. He got her to come to London so he could manipulate her into not telling anyone, especially not telling Eleanor Summerston."

The waiter collected their plates and slipped two dessert menus in place. Jury didn't look; he let Gaby do the looking and didn't bother her with questions until she was done.

"Crème brûlée," she said. "I've always loved crème brûlée."

Like a lover she'd lost who'd come back at last.

"Me too."

When the waiter reappeared, Jury ordered two. "And how about some cognac?"

"I'm half-drunk already." She laughed. The music again.

"There's always the other half." Jury asked for the cognac to be brought later. When the waiter disappeared into the ephemeral light of this restaurant, Jury said, "Manon came back to Paris with the baby?"

Gaby shook her head. "No. I don't know what happened. She did get Gerald Summerston to admit to paternity, if it turned out she was pregnant. Manon was no fool."

"What do you mean?"

"That she wouldn't tell anyone, wouldn't make a fuss, but only if he'd put it in writing to leave the child some part of his fortune; he was very rich, you know."

"And did he?'

"Yes. I have the note he signed."

"So she stayed in Paris for six years without returning to England until now. How did she seem? Excited? Upset? How?" Jury had to wait out this answer for the time it took the waiter to set down their crème brûlée and vanish again.

"Neither one. Manon didn't really show her feelings that way. She was quite calm." Gaby took a bite of the custard and closed her eyes.

No wonder, thought Jury, as he spooned some up. "I don't think I've ever eaten such silken food in my life." But he was so full he couldn't eat any more of the rich dessert and pushed it to one side. "So Manon told you nothing, except about this agreement? You have no idea why she ended up on the tiny island of Bryher?"

"Maybe there was someone she wanted to see there."

"But the only person she knew beside Summerston's wife was dead. Daisy Brownell."

"Daisy . . . that name is familiar, yes." Gaby then said nothing until she'd finished the crème brûlée. She put her spoon down and said, "But that isn't the only person she knew, is it?"

"Who else was there?" Jury was puzzled.

"What about the baby?" She looked at Jury's crème brûlée. "Are you going to eat that?"

PART IV
Bookaboy

30

At the same time Richard Jury was walking the streets of Paris, Melrose Plant was opening his front door—Ruthven being busy with taking tea to the hermitage—to find a lad of perhaps twelve or thirteen with a canvas bag and a determinedly "I'm not buying" look for whatever Melrose was selling. He dropped his canvas bag long enough to pull a bit of paper out of his pocket.

"You this—Mr. Plant, then?"

Suddenly recalling this appointment he'd all but forgotten, Melrose said, "You must be Gerrard."

"Maybe," said Gerrard, covering his bases.

The lad was apparently prepared to debate his own identity. "In the event you are, please come in."

That invitation, with its margin for error, must have satisfied Gerrard, and he entered.

Melrose held out his hand. "I'm Lord Ardry." He tried out the title to see how the boy would take to it.

He didn't. Instead, he again pulled out the crumpled bit of paper, smoothed it, and said, "They told me you was Mr. Melrose Plant."

"I am. You're familiar with titles, I assume?"

"Yeah. That's what you got?" He surveyed the marble foyer. "Nice place. Kind of—ostentatious—that the word?"

"I hope not. It's a word, yes. I bet you like big ones." Melrose gestured toward the living room. "Come on in and have some tea."

"Good idea. I could use a cuppa." He looked almost happy before he hid it.

Taking his usual wing chair, Melrose indicated the chair on the other side of the fireplace, and Gerrard sat down, giving the living room another sweep of his eyes.

"That's some Christmas tree you got there."

"Pretty ostentatious, isn't it?" For indeed it was. The sumptuously decorated tree—over-decorated, Melrose thought—had come from a tree farm just outside of Sidbury. Martha, Ruthven and Pippen had set to work with heirloom crystal balls and figurines; tiny china animals by Herend, Wedgwood and Spode. It would have given Claridge's tree a run for its money, and "money" was what it screamed.

"Nah. It's a Christmas tree. Supposed to be fancy, ain't it? And look at all them fancy presents!" Gerrard let out a soft whistle.

Melrose looked. Most of them had been wrapped by Pippen, who, Melrose was surprised to hear (since Pippen, their new maid, didn't look old enough to have worked anywhere, including here) had held a job in the gift-wrapping department at Harrods. "Quite a stack, I'll admit."

"A lot of money's wrapped up in that lot."

"Right. Incidentally, what's your family name? If your first name's Gerrard."

"Gerrard," he said.

"What? Both names? Gerrard Gerrard?"

"That's it."

"Couldn't your mother have found another first name for you?"

"Too lazy, I expect. We're a lazy lot."

Melrose shook his head. "Not according to the FamilyHire agency. They said you're diligent and hardworking."

"Yeah, I am."

"And they also said you're stubborn, self-centered, arrogant, and demanding." Melrose smiled. "And clever."

"Sounds about right, except for the clever bit."

"And you've got a sense of humor. They didn't tell me that."

"Didn't know, it's my guess. But if I'm stubborn and all that other stuff, why'd you want me?"

"Because I need those excellent qualities to deal with someone else who has them. She's my aunt."

"Yeah. I got one of them, too."

Just then, Ruthven arrived with the heavily-laden tea tray, and Gerrard sat up, arrow-straight.

"Ruthven, this is Gerrard. I told you he'd be staying with us—for how long—?"

"Booked me for two weeks. I could do longer, o' course." He was studying the tea tray when he added that.

To Ruthven, Melrose said, "Perhaps you could show him to his room after tea."

Ruthven bowed. "Certainly, m'lord." He turned to Gerrard. "I hope you enjoy the tea, Master Gerrard."

Gerrard was absolutely wowed. He smiled brightly for the first time. "A butler! Wow! A master, me?"

Far better a butler than an earl. Far better a "Master" than just a Gerrard.

"Okay, back to business," said Melrose, first allowing Gerrard to people up his small plate with everything—scone, cucumber sandwich, egg mayonnaise, cheese and pickle, a little assortment of cakes; a few sitting atop another few as there wasn't room for every occupant to claim a separate place on the plate.

Melrose gave him time to shovel in several of these delicacies before continuing.

"Ordinarily, one of the times this aunt has decreed belongs to her is this—tea time—though not today."

Mouth full, but still managing, the lad said, "So I'm guessing you don't want her joining you. Us. For tea. This here's a real good one. Tea. I ain't used to more'n a cup, me."

Melrose marveled at how quickly the boy had become part of things, watching Gerrard now clamp down on a hard-boiled egg and wondering when eggs had been introduced to the tea assortment. Ruthven and Martha might have decided to protein the boy up. Gerrard did look a little pale and undernourished. Melrose corrected the "ain't." "*Not* used to more than."

"I gotta start talking like you, then?"

"Not for my sake, no. But your own sake might be worth thinking about."

Gerrard, scone in hand, put his head back and closed his eyes, as if having a think.

"Not right now, for heaven's sakes."

Gerrard sat forward again and put more jam on his scone. "Do we eat dinner, too? I mean after this lot?"

"We do indeed. But later. You must be getting stuffed, though. Hardly enough room for another meal."

"I always got room, thanks." He drank off his tea, replaced his cup, shot out his arms. "Great!"

Melrose pushed the button beneath the tabletop and Ruthven returned. "Show Master Gerrard to his room, will you, Ruthven?"

"Sir." Ruthven picked up the canvas carryall.

"Ah, wait, Mr. Ruthven. I can do that."

"Not at all, Master Gerrard. And it's just 'Ruthven.'"

"Seems kind of disrespectful," said Gerrard, as they moved to the foyer and the stairs, making remarks Melrose understood to be, "I really liked them—those—eggs. Where'd you get 'em?"

"From a chicken, Master Gerrard."

Gerrard laughed hard and said, "A comedian butler! Mr. Ruthven, I'm stayin."

It appeared that Mr. Ruthven and Master Gerrard were a lock.

31

When Gerrard came back downstairs for dinner at eight, looking shiny as a brand-new button, it was evident Ruthven had been hard at work.

Gerrard's jacket and pants, though mismatched, had been carefully brushed and his white shirt pressed. Around the collar of the shirt he wore a polka-dot bow tie.

Agatha was in the living room and was introduced to "my cousin— second or probably third, as his father's the actual cousin." Whereupon, Agatha stood aghast and agape. Melrose took note of "agape," for it might come in handy if he got another goat.

"Cousin? Cousin?" She said it a third time: "*Cousin?*" Being in locked-in-cousin syndrome, she did not take the hand that Gerrard politely extended. "But you—" she addressed Melrose, "—don't have—"

"A cousin? Oh, but I do. I've just never mentioned the family. The Gerrards of London." As if all London were bowled over by the name. "It's just been so long since I've seen them."

Gerrard should not have taken "clever" out of the mix, for he was as good at filling in blanks, at making deductions from minimal information, as Marshall Trueblood.

"Dad was afraid you'd forgotten him. You know, Ben."

"Forget Ben Gerrard? Never. Not in a million years. Though it's certainly bad of me that I've seen so little of you all. How long's it been . . . ?" Melrose looked at Gerrard for help.

"Dad says maybe twelve years."

"Oh, surely not. A few London visits ago, I'm sure I stopped by to say hello. Your family being my only *blood relations*, after all."

Although Agatha was physically immobile, Melrose knew "blood" would have her mind racing at the speed of light, or at least of the wind that had raked the wheat fields around Dorothy's cottage and spun Dorothy and Toto into the sky, as it now threatened to pull all of the beautiful objects in Ardry End with it, together with the house itself, which it would then drop *plunk* into the Munchkinland of North London.

"If it was all them years ago, you never even seen—saw—three of us kids—" Gerrard turned to Agatha with that bit of divvying-up-the-inheritance news, and then made it worse: "There's six altogether." Back to Melrose. "Let me tell you, to live in a place like this—oh, no disrespect, Cousin Melrose. We ain't lookin' forward to—you know—none of us wants to see you—" He put his hand to his neck in a throttling gesture. "You know."

Wrong. One of us does and she's sitting right opposite you.

Gerrard went on to talk about the size of Ardry End, how grand it was, all of these big windows and fires and mantel-pieces. If horror could be said to double, triple, quadruple, like vodka and vermouth in a De-morney martini—if horror could move in waves coming more quickly upon them like the walking dead—Agatha's expression moved from abject to absolute to all-engulfing as she drank what must have been her fourth sherry. Ruthven stood with the decanter ready with refills.

Melrose was gazing through the top of the high window at a moon that looked newly minted, wanting only a starry bow tie to join the party.

"And to think," Gerrard went on happily, "we each of us gets his own toilet!"

Agatha choked.

Moonlight and marble and toilets. Melrose marveled. It was wonderful not to have to do the work himself, to have someone else make it all up. Gerrard, he decided, should get another grand. Maybe two.

"And not to worry, Mr. Ruthven, you and your fam'ly, they'll be all right."

It came out "fambly."

Delightfully, Ruthven took it up. "Master Gerrard, my own fambly consists of just myself and my wife, Martha."

"Yeah, but there must be other maids and stuff in a place like this. And all that big garden out back."

"Indeed, there are maids and stuff. There's the groundskeeper. There's even a hermit. I expect you'll want him to stay." Ruthven laughed a little as he poured Agatha another sherry.

Had she still been sober, Agatha would have grabbed up the cigarette-lighter gun and shot the kid where he sat. Then reloaded and made her way to London to pick off Ben and all the other Gerrards.

Gerrard was starting in again, and Melrose interrupted to avoid having to call Medical Alert and all of them having to go to the ER. "Well, Ruthven, I expect dinner must be about ready."

"Indeed, sir. I'll just see Martha."

Who will not be out of a job when I pack it in, I'm glad to hear.

"Oh, boy, what's for din-dins?" said Gerrard.

"The best food you've ever eaten." He rose when Ruthven returned to announce dinner. "Gerrard would like to know what we're having, Ruthven."

"Beef tenderloin, m'lord."

"Roast, is it?" said Gerrard.

"Indeed, Master Gerrard. With browned potatoes."

Gerrard grinned and rubbed his hands together as he rose from his chair.

Agatha remained locked in her seat. Melrose wondered if they'd have to pick up the chair to get her into the dining room.

But, no. It was a struggle, but she made it to the best food Gerrard had ever eaten in the best dining room he would ever inherit.

PART V
Comeback

32

When Melrose walked into the dining room for breakfast the following morning, Gerrard was already seated at the table, his plate full of the offerings from the silver dishes lined up on the buffet. Indeed, judging by the heaped-up plate, Melrose wondered if there were any offerings left. Not that he really cared, as he didn't himself eat most of the stuff there.

"Mornin', Mel," said Gerrard, happily.

Mel? "Good morning, Gerrard. I see the breakfast is to your liking."

This flight into sarcasm was as present to Gerrard as a first-class flight on Emirates. "Lemme tell you, that Mrs. Ruthven cooks up the best breakfast I ever seen—saw. This here's my second helping."

Ruthven entered with Melrose's tea. "Thanks, Ruthven. Gerrard was just complimenting Martha's breakfast."

"Indeed. Would you care for some more tea, Master Gerrard?"

"I would that, Mr. Ruthven, ta very much." He shoved his cup forward. Ruthven poured.

"Tell me something, Gerrard," said Melrose. "It's 'Mr. Ruthven,' when technically it should be just 'Ruthven'; it's 'Mrs. Ruthven,' when technically it should be 'Martha.' But it's just plain 'Mel,' when technically it should be 'Mr. Plant.'"

"Ah, come on, Mel. We're mates, that's why." Gerrard winked.

Melrose, although he was now feeling kind of matey, did not return the wink.

"So ain—aren't—you going to get some eggs and sausages?" Gerrard pointed with his fork in case Mel might not know where to find them.

"My regular breakfast is a little different . . . and here it comes."

Ruthven set down the buttered toast and the boiled egg in an egg-cup unlike the usual silver one. This one Melrose hadn't used since he was a toddler. Melrose asked him, "Did you get hold of Treadwell?"

"Indeed, sir. Mr. Treadwell said he would be glad to come to Northamptonshire this morning and should be arriving shortly." Ruthven was looking at the longcase clock.

"Would ya look at that!" said Gerrard, nodding at Melrose's breakfast. "That eggcup has some kinda fella holding a hammer and a spoon."

"To crack it open and to eat it. Notice, too, the round hat. That keeps the egg warm."

"My God, Mel. That's for a kid-like."

"I am kid-like." He proceeded to cut his toast into oblongs.

"You ain't making soldiers?"

"I always do," Melrose said as the doorbell gave its dulcet ring. He was trying to use the tiny hammer to crack the egg, but found it clumsy going. There! He peeled the shell down a little and, as Ruthven hadn't supplied the silver egg-spoon, he had to gouge it with the play-spoon. "Just right," he said to a fascinated Gerrard, as he dipped into it with one of the toast pieces.

At that point, Agatha, walking straight through Ruthven's announcement of her, entered. She was hauling a large book that Melrose recognized as *Burke's Peerage*. It was probably his own copy of *Burke's*, though he couldn't imagine how she could have got it out of his library without his knowing. He knew only what it meant and, after she was settled at the table with her cup of tea and a biscuit, butter and jam, she began.

"As you see, I've been dipping into *Burke's*—"

Melrose loved the familiarity of that address.

"—and was surprised to see that the Ardry–Plant line has no mention of a Gerrard, nor any name resembling it." Here she cast a smug look at Gerrard, across the table from her.

Gerrard was unflappable. "O'course not. Me great-great-great-great-grandfather would of changed his own name after that William Bloone got called up before just about ev'ry magistrate in London for things like nickin' silver, car thieving, impersonating an officer of the law, and who knows what else? Yeah, they was a bad lot, that part of the fam'ly, and my great-great-et-cetera-grandad didn't want them blotting the fam'ly name, so the 'Gerrard' name got added later. Prob'ly too late to get into that book."

This reasoning was so inane Melrose knew Agatha wouldn't be able to question it, but she did ask, "Well, what was the name originally?" She was opening the volume to her bookmarked spot as the doorbell sounded again.

"Dunno. You don't expect me to remember that? I can ask me da though and get back to you."

Ruthven entered then, his expression suggesting his lordship had never had such a cartload of fun as was to be had right now. He announced the arrival not only of Superintendent Richard Jury but also of Mr. Treadwell, of Yarborough, Seward and Treadwell, Melrose's law firm.

"Richard!" Melrose's astonishment was no match for Agatha's.

"Mr. *Treadwell*!"

She didn't care about the police, only about the possible alteration of wills and subsequent inheritances.

"Madam," said Mr. Treadwell. No "Lady Ardry" here.

Jury was introduced to Gerrard, who, if he hadn't been in heaven with all his buttered eggs, sausages and kippers, went straight to it now. "Scotland Yard! Wow-ow!" Not only did Scotland Yard beat an earl, it beat a butler.

As Jury wandered back to the sideboard, he said, "Nice to meet you, Gerrard. I hope you didn't eat everything."

"There's sausages left, and a bit of that kipper."

Jury forked up both and went to the table and took the chair next to Gerrard.

Melrose, out of respect for the elderly Mr. Treadwell, was still standing. "Mr. Treadwell, could I get you anything? Coffee? Tea?"

"Tea would be welcome, thank you."

"And this is Gerrard. My cousin. Or to be more exact, his father, Benjamin Gerrard, is my cousin."

Mr. Treadwell, trained to accept client surprises, said simply, "I wasn't aware you had relations still living, Lord Ardry."

"Nor were any of us!" said Agatha. "Except, of course, for me."

"I was speaking," said Mr. Treadwell as Ruthven poured his tea, "of blood relations."

Scripted, it couldn't have been better. Melrose thought he heard a thunderclap as Agatha regarded Gerrard.

"Well, I can understand that you might want to make a few changes," said Mr. Treadwell, careful not to actually refer to Melrose's will.

Melrose was close to believing there actually was a cousin. He rose and said, "Mr. Treadwell, if we could just have a word in the library. Ruthven will bring us more tea."

"Of course." Mr. Treadwell rose and they left the table.

As soon as Melrose had set his solicitor straight, and Ruthven had seen him to his car where he had a driver waiting, Jury left Agatha to *Burke's Peerage* and Gerrard and went into the library.

"That argument—assuming there was one—Flora Flood had with her husband before she shot him—"

"She didn't do it."

Jury sighed. "All right. What I'm wondering is what Bub overheard but is denying, and whether maybe another kid can get it out of him."

"The only kid I know is Gerrard."

"That's what I mean. He's clever."

"Too clever by half."

"Take him to Watermeadows, why don't you, while Flora Flood is in London for a couple days."

"You mean now?"

Jury nodded. Then he told Melrose about his Paris visit and what Gabrielle Belrose had said about Manon and Gerald Summerston.

"My Lord! That certainly puts a different face upon things, wouldn't you say?"

"Indeed."

"But Bryher? She comes to England and goes to Bryher? You think it had something to do with the baby?"

"God knows *something* had to do with the baby. I'm going to Bryher tomorrow. You can go with me. You'd be helpful in reducing the police presence."

"Why doesn't that sound like a compliment?"

"Because it isn't?" Jury smiled. "Oh, come on, you're really good with children."

"What? Are you mad? They can't stand me. Unless I'm part of their little plot. Where do you think all of this is leading?"

"I'd say to Tony Servino."

Melrose looked surprised. "Servino?"

"From what we've heard about Gerald Summerston, far from being the soul of kindness, I'd say he needed a fixer."

Following Jury's departure, Melrose herded Gerrard into the Bentley and they set off for Watermeadows, Gerrard protesting this excursion to meet "some little kid."

"You're 'some little kid' too, so stop complaining." Melrose braked to avoid hitting a cow that didn't seem to want to leave the road.

"You nearly hit that cow, Mel; watch your driving."

"I'm close to nearly hitting you, Gerrard. Watch your talk."

* * *

Watermeadows brought forth numerous *wow*s from Gerrard, and the comment that it was even better than Ardry End.

"Except," said Melrose getting out of the car, "you're not inheriting it. Come on."

It was the cook who answered the door, her apron floured and smeared with chocolate, and who informed Melrose that Miss Flora had gone to London, but that yes, little Bub was there, upstairs in his room. "Just run on up," she said to Gerrard.

"Run on up" struck Melrose as a rather careless direction, since the cook didn't know what articles along the way Gerrard might stick under his shirt—nor did Gerrard show any propensity to run to meet Bub. "Third room on the left," said the cook, taking his hesitation as indication he didn't know where to run to.

"Go ahead," said Melrose. "I'll wait for you down here in the library."

The cook kindly brought him in some tea and he was standing, drinking from his cup, when he heard laughter overhead and saw, up on the little balcony, Gerrard and Bub wielding the pole the maid used to pull the chandelier towards the balcony. Melrose told them to cut it out, and, reluctantly, they did.

"You ready to go?" he called up to Gerrard.

"Okay." Gerrard said a few words to Bub and the next thing Melrose knew, he was in the library. "The kid knows how to have fun." He was looking up at the chandelier. "I'll say that for him."

"I won't," said Melrose. "Let's go."

They stopped by the kitchen where Melrose poked his head round the door and thanked the cook for the tea.

"Find out anything?" he asked Gerrard.

"Nah," said Gerrard. "Except he really liked Tony. And the fight was started not by him but by Flora. Who I kind of get the impression he's not all that crazy about."

33

A half hour following their return to Ardry End, Melrose looked out of the longcase window facing his drive to see a red Ferrari parked there. He called for Ruthven, who came immediately.

"Ruthven, whose car is that?"

"Mr. Rice's, m'lord. He arrived whilst you were out in the library and asked me not to bother you. He's come to see Miss Sydney. Or rather, she'd asked him to come."

"And where are—"

"In the stables, sir. Mr. Rice came to the kitchen a while ago to ask me to call—"

Melrose didn't wait for the call, but headed toward the rear of the house. "That's where I'll be," he called back over his shoulder.

*   *   *

"Vernon! Nice to see you. I didn't know—" He stopped talking when he saw Sydney's tear-stained face and the handkerchief she quickly applied to it. "What's wrong?"

Vernon answered for her. "Sydney's feeling very bad. She's waiting for her grandfather. I asked Ruthven to ring him at the farm and to ask him to come, which he said he would do right away."

"But what *happened*?"

In a choked voice, Sydney said, "It's nothing to do with you or Ardry End. Can we wait for Granddad?"

"Of course. But come into the house."

She shook her head. "I'd rather be out here with Aggrieved. And Vernon. Please."

The wait wasn't long. Thirty minutes later, Tom Brownell was there in the stable, looking bewildered. "Sydney?"

She opened her mouth to speak, but nothing came out. She turned to Vernon, gave him an imploring look, but he shook his head. Then, looking at her downturned face, changed his mind and spoke. "It's about her mum, Tom. She'll tell you."

"About Daisy, sweetheart? What?"

Sydney began weeping, saying through the tears, "I'm so sorry, Granddad. I'm so—" But the tears overcame the telling.

In his calm voice, Tom said, "Never mind, Sydney. Nothing's so bad you can't tell me."

"This is! I killed Mum; I mean, I'm afraid I killed her; no, I know it. Mum hadn't told you this because she didn't want you to worry yet, Grandad, but she was quite ill. There was a nurse, Anna, who was staying with us to care for her. But that night Anna had an emergency at the hospital and had to leave and told me just as she was going to be careful of giving Mum any pain pills. 'In another hour, no more than two, Sydney. No more.' It was less than an hour when Mum asked for more because of the pain. So I gave her two. But then in a few minutes she asked for more, said that the pain was unbearable. I told her I couldn't; that Anna had said only two. But Mum kept asking and finally begging and holding on to my hand and—well, you know Mummy never complained about stuff, so this was so—I tried to call Anna at the hospital but couldn't get hold of her and Mum was—" The weeping took Sydney over. "So—"

"You gave her some more. Sydney, it's all right; what could you do?"

"Be stronger! Be able to step back from it. Oh, God! I'm so sorry, Granddad." She turned not to her grandfather but to Aggrieved and lay her head against his flank.

Tom put his hand on her shoulder. "We don't even know if that was enough of an overdose to kill her. But look at it this way, sweetheart, what we do know is that she didn't deliberately kill herself, and God knows that's a relief." He hugged her.

What he'd just said calmed her. "I didn't think . . . Yes, that's true."

Melrose knew that Tom Brownell had always known Daisy hadn't committed suicide, but it was a good reason to come up with for Sydney's sake.

"Thanks, Vernon," said Sydney. "Thank you." But it wasn't Vernon she was patting; it was the horse.

"I was nothing but a sounding board, Sydney, and not as good a one as your horse." Vernon laughed.

The inimitable Vernon Rice, thought Melrose. He remembered how Vernon had handled Nell Ryder. When Nell reappeared that day after having been gone for two years, it was Vernon Rice she had gone to, not her grandfather. He had that effect on people. The one you could always trust.

Absently, Sydney picked up a brush and started brushing Aggrieved. "But you knew," she said. "Not precisely *what,* but that I felt guilty and you put that together with Mum."

"You still talking to Aggrieved?"

She turned and looked at Vernon. "No. To you. You knew."

Vernon threw up his hands. "I'm happy to have you think I can read your mind, but—"

"You can. You knew."

Melrose looked at Vernon and thought about Nell. Sydney was right. He knew.

34

Having returned to the drawing room, Melrose heard the doorbell and once again, in the absence of Ruthven, got out of his wing chair and opened the door. There he was confronted by a stranger, a tallish man wearing sunglasses and a trilby hat. Melrose especially liked this getup this time of year.

"Mr. Plant?"

"Yes. May I help you?" This was to be, apparently, a red-hot day for visitors to Ardry End.

The man removed his glasses, held out his hand and said, "Jenks. George Jenks. How do you do?"

Melrose shook his hand, still wondering whose hand he shook. The name meant nothing to him.

Reading his mind, Jenks said, "Means nothing to you, I know, but I hear you have a great horse."

Melrose took a surprised step back. "I do? You've an interest in my horse?"

George Jenks nodded. "I'm a trainer." He repeated his name. "Jenks."

"Oh? And do I need a trainer?"

Jenks was by now inside and Ruthven had returned, followed by Vernon and Sydney. Ruthven was taking Jenks's coat.

Vernon's eyes widened. "*George* Jenks?"

Everyone else in the world had apparently heard of George Jenks: Vernon, Sydney, and possibly Aggrieved himself.

"Mr. Jenks," said Vernon, "is one of the country's greatest trainers." He extended his hand. "We've met, but you probably don't remember. At Ryder Stables outside of Cambridge. How did you hear about Aggrieved?"

"A mutual friend—" he smiled at Melrose "—got in touch with me. Said your horse was a very good horse."

Sydney said, "He is. A really good horse. But I didn't know—" She turned to Melrose. "That you intended to race him."

"Nor did I," said Melrose.

George Jenks laughed. "Do you suppose I could see this horse?"

"Of course," said Melrose, "but tell me about this mutual—"

"Come on with us," said Sydney.

The three of them sailed off to the stable, leaving Melrose in the questionable company of the mutual friend.

Gerrard was out there now, giving Aggrieved a rubdown.

"Take him out of the stable," said Sydney, "so Mr. Jenks can see him."

Gerrard looked as if he might debate this choice, but shrugged and led Aggrieved out.

Jenks took a long look at his head, then ran his hand across the horse's flank. Gently, he dug his fingers into the shoulder, then the hip, stood back and studied the horse from different angles. He said, "Good-looking horse." But he said it much too matter-of-factly for Gerrard.

"'Good-looking?' That's all? This here horse is beautiful."

Jenks nodded. "You take good care of him, son."

Taking issue with this, Sydney said, "Actually, I'm pretty much the caretaker."

"And doing a fine job. Where can we ride? Is there a ring?"

Melrose, who'd come out to the barns, was pleased to announce that yes, there was. He hadn't known it himself until Ruthven had enlightened him. Melrose's father had put in a ring years before for a future of Melrose's riding. He had never fulfilled that future, since he had not liked to ride, hadn't even liked his pony. His father had said that of course one day he would have to ride to hounds. Whereupon his mother had said, "Why?" Melrose had always loved the way his beloved and sensible mother could cut his father off at the knees with no more than the simple question "Why?"

In no mood for trooping, still Melrose had followed the little party, trooping through the woods with Gerrard leading Aggrieved. No wonder he hadn't known about the ring, buried as it was from view by oaks and chestnuts, and farther from the house than Melrose ever ventured, anyway. He was quite indifferent to his own property, property meaning little to him, whereas heritage meant a lot.

"Kind of stingy," said Gerrard. "You should keep it up better, Mel." He was positioning blanket and saddle on Aggrieved's back.

"Indeed? Well, I didn't know Mr. Jenks was coming, or I'd have had Blodgett out here with his rake and blower—and who delegated you to do the riding? What about Sydney?"

They quarreled over this for a while until George Jenks interrupted. "Do you mind if I have a go at it?"

They both, or rather the three of them, looked slightly astounded. "You?" said Melrose.

"Trainers do know how to ride, Mr. Plant. It's necessary. Do you mind?"

"Oh. Of course not."

Jenks did not heave himself into the saddle, nor fling himself in. The movement was more in the nature of being a takeoff, the sort that a small plane or a bird might make. But once up there, it was clear he belonged. He made small clicking sounds in his mouth, and Aggrieved reacted as if he'd been hearing those sounds since the day he was born and ventured into the ring and started walking, then went from a walk to a trot to a gallop. Then faster.

"Wow!" said Gerrard and Sydney, together.

After going once round the track, Jenks slowed the horse down, trotted it over to where the others stood, and dismounted. "Very nice horse," he said, handing the reins back to Gerrard.

Who frowned. "Not very excitable, are you? That horse was going damned fast."

Jenks smiled a little. "Not as fast as he could have done. I had to restrain him."

"You did?" Gerrard was astonished. "What's the fastest horse ever?"

George Jenks thought about this for a few moments. "Hard to decide on one. But probably Secretariat. A combination of his stride, his heart, his metabolism. They were not only great in and of themselves, they came together seamlessly. If you can think of the phrase in a positive sense, Secretariat was a perfect storm."

35

Jenks having left, with a promise to return to talk about training, Melrose told Ruthven he was going out.

"Out" not being much of a destination in Long Piddleton, he wound up heading for the Jack and Hammer with Vivian, Joanna, Diane, Trueblood and the unwelcome Theo Wrenn Brown.

Diane was holding forth about drugs in horse racing. "He was up before the Horseracing Authority disciplinary board several times. A hypo found in his kit in the stables before the Oaks. It was Bork Sands's own horse, something called Silver Sands, I think."

"Diane," said Melrose, "where do you get all of this horse-racing arcana? Who's Bork Sands?"

At just that point the door of the Jack and Hammer's saloon bar opened and to Melrose's surprise George Jenks walked in. Walked in and walked over to their table, bent down and kissed Diane Demorney on her cheek.

If there is such a thing as a communal gasp, the other five occupants of the table gasped it.

"Hello, sweetheart," said George to Diane.

Sweetheart?

"Hello, Georgie."

Georgie? Sweetheart? A communal jaw-drop.

When George lay his arm across the back of Diane's chair, had the others allowed themselves a rude response, they would have whipped out their phones and clicked a picture.

Mrs. Withersby, however, unconcerned about rudeness and having no camera, resorted to mop and mouth. "Bloody hell!" she said loudly as her mop dropped out of its two inches of water, which water spread over Theo Wrenn Brown's shoe.

Diane introduced him: "George Jenks, my ex-husband."

Communal crash of mugs and glasses on table.

George laughed. "But I'm only one of them."

"The others not being welcome," said Diane, plugging a cigarette into her holder, which George then lit.

"Sorry to interrupt," he said to the table in general. Then, to Melrose, and looking at Diane, he said, "The mutual friend."

"We were talking about horses and drugs. Did you ever hear of a trainer named Bork Sands?" said Diane.

"The Borkster?" said George with a laugh. "Sure, only he wasn't a trainer. He was a vet."

"A horse vet? What stables did he work for?"

"Different ones. Mainly the Summerston stables." He turned to Diane. "You remember that horse Epiphany? Won the St. Leger? Won a lot of races for such a mediocre horse." George smiled. "That horse couldn't've made it out of the backstretch without a great jockey and God."

"Are you saying," said Joanna Lewes, "the horse won because he was drugged?"

"No, but you don't hire Bork Sands just to get rid of stable cough."

"Still," said Trueblood, "the drugging could happen without the owner knowing, couldn't it?"

George looked at Trueblood as if he were either crazy or five years old. "But why would it?"

"Then someone must have suspected."

"Not necessarily. Look, I'm not claiming the horse was drugged. I'm only saying that Summerston would have known if the horse *had* been. It would have been a hell of a scandal if it got out."

"Could it still be?"

Puzzled, they all looked at him. "What?"

"A scandal? Have you ever seen that gossip column in one of the tabloid rags called Comeback? It's not about some entertainer's fresh success, it's old gossip—old stuff the columnist brings back from months or even years ago. Bits of things that were never resolved. A few days ago there was something about Summerston's war record: he got the something-for-gallantry award. Well, someone claimed that he hadn't really done the thing that earned it, something about grabbing up a machine gun and keeping a North Korean unit from shooting his men. This chap who's disputing Summerston's part says it was his own father who'd saved the men. He wants the Queen to revoke the award and give it to his father."

"Can that be done? *Would* it be done?" said Vivian.

"Why not?" said Trueblood. "Awards have been rescinded all over the place. For all kinds of reasons: criminal conviction; unworthy conduct; men stripped of titles for scandals involving money, sex, et cetera. Certainly for misrepresentation of bravery in the service."

"That'd play hell with a man's reputation if it got out," said Melrose, recalling Jury's comment about Summerston needing a fixer.

PART VI
Black Swan

36

Macalvie had sent a car for them to Exeter Airport, and Jury and Plant were now walking into his office. Or rather pushing their way in, as Gilly Thwaite was rushing out of it, looking not at all pleased.

Tom Brownell was sitting in one of the chairs across from Macalvie's desk. Macalvie was marking up pages in a folder that he tossed aside when Jury and Plant came in. Beside his desk sat a large stuffed giraffe.

"Who's that?"

Macalvie looked at the giraffe as if he weren't sure. "Oh, him? That's Jerome. He's the new head of SOCO. Gilly Thwaite just quit. As you might have noticed, she's displeased with the replacement."

"Hello, Tom," said Melrose.

Tom nodded. "You're going to Bryher? He's yours to take along."

"Why do I not feel in need of a giraffe?"

"Don't know. But you'll reduce the threat of police presence with it."

"And why am I always to be some sort of corrective for 'police presence'? Rather than merely being a distraction, it would be nice to be known for making a contribution."

Macalvie pulled over another folder. "Yeah. So let us know when you make one. Tom here thinks you'll get something out of Zillah about the night of the shooting if you can approach the subject with, ah—"

"Giraffe-speak?" said Jury.

Tom laughed. "Not only Zillah, but it'll throw off Zoe, at least long enough that Zillah can say something about the woman on the beach. Maybe."

"Well, then you ought to come, too, Tom."

Tom shook his head. "Police presence, remember? Three of us would be entirely too many. Anyway, I'm going to visit Dr. Park." He looked at Jury. "Howe Park. The doctor who wasn't at the foundling hospital when we visited. But who was apparently in charge when I think Manon Vinet was there six years ago."

"Right," said Macalvie, "so why don't you guys get your skates on? Incidentally, the medical records have come through on Moira." He spoke to Tom. "You wanted to know if—"

"If she'd had an abortion."

Macalvie raised his eyebrows. "Good guess. Yeah. She had." When Tom made no comment, he went on: "Enlighten me later. Meanwhile, I'll get someone to drive you to the airport." He called out to Effie, who poked her head in, and he gave her that assignment. "No, I don't mean you, Effie. Find someone who knows how to drive."

*   *   *

The Skybus headed for St. Mary's with the giraffe sitting on a jump seat.

As the three of them left the plane to board the ferry to Bryher, Jury said, "We look ridiculous."

"We often do."

"Correction: *You* often do. I manage to avoid it."

"Not this time," said Melrose.

Hilda Noyes, after a visit from "that *nice* Mr. Brownell—" was no longer put off by police presence in her home, even police accompanied by a giraffe.

Jury introduced Plant and asked if they could speak to the girls.

They were both there, almost magically, at that. Zoe held tight to Zillah's hand. But Melrose could see Zillah's mouth drop open and her eyes round out.

"Could we sit down, Mrs. Noyes?"

She motioned them into the chair and loveseat across from the sofa. Melrose took the loveseat and sat the giraffe beside him.

"And Zoe and Zillah, too?" said Jury.

"Well, I don't know—"

But her not-knowing had no effect on the girls, especially Zillah, who took, in the movement toward seating, the opportunity to yank her hand from Zoe's. She then displaced the giraffe beside Melrose and sat down herself and pulled the giraffe closer.

"Mrs. Noyes," said Jury.

"Yes?"

"Zillah, as a baby, was brought to you by—?"

"A friend of her mother. Just a baby, Zillah would not remember her—"

"But I would," exclaimed Zoe. "I was nearly eight."

Jury turned to Zoe. "And was she the woman you saw on the beach?"

Zoe just shook and shook her head.

"Do you remember Mrs. Cooke, Zoe?" said Jury.

Zoe flinched. "She's dead."

"You told me about her," said Zillah.

"Be quiet, Zillah!" Then to Jury, she said, "Yes, I remember her."

"What about the woman from the beach. Do you remember her?"

"I don't know what you're talking about."

"Yes you do. You're the one who got her to the beach."

Zoe tossed her hair. "How'd I do that? I didn't even know her."

"But you knew who she was because I'll bet you read the letter she'd written Mrs. Noyes in which she said she was coming to England, to Bryher. I think your aunt gave you a message to take to the Hell Bay just before Manon Vinet came. That note probably told Ms. Vinet that Hilda Noyes would come to the hotel at a certain time and they'd meet there." Jury paused and glanced at Hilda Noyes, whose face looked to have turned hard as stone.

Zoe said nothing.

"Come on, Zoe. Your aunt is sitting right here. You simply typed up another note and signed Hilda Noyes's name."

Zoe still said nothing, but Zillah, clutching the giraffe, said, "You said she was a witch, you said—"

"Shut up, Zillah! Next, you'll be saying I shot her. Where would I ever have got a gun?"

"From Jack Couch, in exchange for your father's SIG Sauer P226," said Jury.

Zoe looked at Zillah and fairly screamed out the words: "It's all your fault, you know that, don't you? Now what's going to happen—?"

Hilda Noyes was growing increasingly upset by this exchange between the girls. "Zoe, are you saying you two went to the beach looking for someone that night?"

"No, Aunt Hilda. Zillah's making it all up."

"I'm not! You were the one who told me the lady was some kind of witch!"

Zoe turned on Zillah eyes of ice and an expression so full of ire Jury felt his blood run cold. Had he been six years old, it would have scared him into speechlessness, too.

Zillah was nearly strangling the giraffe with the grip she had on it. Jury put his arms round both her and the giraffe. "It's all right, Zillah. Nothing to be scared of. The lady you saw was just a lady; no witches, no ghosts. Don't cry."

She was weeping loudly, her body now pressed half against Jury, half against the giraffe. Jury looked up and signed to Plant, who kneeled down and took his place, while Jury rose and went to Zoe, who said, "She was going to take Zillah away."

"I know," said Jury. "She was Zillah's mum. She'd waited years to come and get her."

"But Zillah's mine. She's mine! I've been with her since after she was born! It's not fair that someone can just take her away. Zillah spent her whole babyhood with me. I just wanted to tell that woman that she couldn't have Zillah, but when we got there she was dead!"

Her whole babyhood. Jury thought it one of the saddest little descriptions he'd ever heard. And this child Zoe looked flattened, looked empty, as if all the breath had been drawn out of her.

37

"Inspector Brownell," said Dr. Howe Park, "I don't believe there's anything I can tell you."

They were sitting in the doctor's office in his home in St. Just.

"I'm not trying to violate your confidentiality obligations, Dr. Park, but I think there might be a few things you could tell me. The baby was kept at the Summerston shelter with her mother for two weeks, you said, then released to a friend of the mother. Someone I imagine you knew."

"Why would you think that?"

"Because Summerston is a private hospital that operates, or certainly did at the time, for the personal benefit of the Summerstons, consequently for people connected with them."

"That's not true; it takes in homeless, ill, or otherwise-in-need people."

"It's the 'otherwise-in-need' I'm talking about. The friend, the woman who took the baby, was well known on Bryher: Daisy Cooke."

Park's expression was a dead giveaway.

"And as both of these women now are dead, I don't think it would be violating confidentiality to tell me about the child. And as you know, this child's mother, Manon Vinet, was murdered. So any information at all you could give me would help us find her killer."

The doctor went back to his chair. "Inspector, all that I know is that the child was given over to Mrs. Cooke. But after that, I can't say what happened to her. Perhaps Mrs. Cooke formally adopted her."

"No, she didn't."

"If you're sure of that, why, then, don't you know—?"

"Mrs. Cooke was my daughter."

38

O
n his way from St. Just to Land's End, Tom rang Jury on his mobile. "Where are you now?"

"Just about to board the plane back to Land's End."

"I've been in St. Just, so I'm nearly there. Let's meet at the Old Success and compare notes."

"Haven't got any notes. I do have a theory, though it's a bit of a black swan theory. Hold on." Tom waited. "Plant also has his idea on this, with which I disagree, although he says it's better than mine, more of a grey swan."

"Really? And Jerome?"

"Who?"

"Your giraffe. Doesn't he have a theory?"

"Oh, we left Jerome with Zillah. She was ever so happy."

"Well, she better watch it. He's bigger than she is. See you soon."

* * *

In the Old Success, the three of them had just got their pints set before them when Tom said, "Dr. Park was not giving much up. But when I mentioned Daisy, his silence told me I was on track. Turns out she took the baby from the foundling hospital."

"Lines up, we know it was Daisy who left the baby in Hilda Noyes's care. But never really left her. Daisy was checking in with Hilda for years. The years before—" Jury stopped, not wanting to say "she died."

But Tom remained unflappable. "She would do. Daisy would do that for a woman in Manon Vinet's position, even though she barely knew her. Daisy was like that."

"I know," said Jury. When Tom looked at him dubiously, Jury merely repeated it. "Believe me, I know."

Tom dropped it and said, "Let's hear these theories. He looked at Jury. "Your theory?"

"Zoe Noyes."

"My God! That'd definitely be a black swan event. She's what? Fourteen years old?"

Jury nodded. "It wouldn't be the first time a kid had killed somebody, Tom. And she had a hell of a motive. Manon Vinet was coming to take Zillah away. For Zoe, that would be like taking her own child away. She said as much. Zillah had been with her since she was a baby. And Zoe substituted her own note for her aunt's that got Manon to the beach. Zillah was scared to death. Zoe as good as admitted that she had a gun."

Tom held up his hand. "Wait a minute. Where would Zoe get a gun?"

"Zoe had her father's old SIG Sauer. There's a collector on Bryher, Jack Couch, who really wanted it. They could have orchestrated a little trade."

"No halfway responsible adult would make an exchange like that."

"Maybe Jack isn't all that responsible."

"Then you're settling on two shooters, because I see no way Zoe could have shot Tony Servino. Or Moira Quinn. Even if there were a motive, which I can't see, either."

"I agree. There must have been two shooters," said Jury.

Tom looked at Melrose. "And yours?"

Melrose said, "Eleanor Summerston. Don't look like that," he said to Jury. "She's the one with the most motive I've heard so far. It's Gerald Summerston's reputation. Lady Summerston would do anything to protect that, certainly get rid of Tony Servino, whom she hated anyway, and who'd probably been hired by Gerald to fix whatever needed to be, including this demand about the gallantry medal. It wouldn't have aroused anyone's suspicions if they'd seen Eleanor at Watermeadows that evening; after all, she owns the place. Eleanor was a keen shooter, better than the men who came to the weekend shooting parties. You didn't notice the pictures on the wall of the library?

"As to shooting Manon Vinet, of course she could have done. Anyone who could wield a shotgun as she could, could certainly manage a handgun. I'd say she saw the Vinet woman at the hotel and for old times' sake had a little drink with her, then suggested a little walk. Shot her on the beach."

Tom grunted. "That's possible. But then what about Moira Quinn? She was only the Summerstons' maid. I suppose pregnant maid, as it turns out."

"Eleanor was so convinced of her husband's egalitarianism, and she knew of his special fondness for maids, maybe she suspected . . ."

"That doesn't sound likely, though," said Tom.

"And she was there at the same time Manon Vinet was there. Lady Summerston could have feared that she'd discovered that relationship."

Tom shook his head. "Aren't both of you ignoring the obvious?"

Jury and Plant exchanged looks. "Such as?"

"The white swan. Flora Flood."

When both of them just stared at him, Tom said, "Flora Flood was the one holding the gun, after all. Wouldn't she have had even more reason than Eleanor Summerston to kill Tony Servino? She adored Gerald and hated Tony for leaving her for Daisy. Flora is not a person to accept rejection."

"But the second shot—" said Melrose.

"She takes a few steps back toward the French door and fires the gun again and then claims an "intruder."

"But Bryher? Why didn't police suspect her?"

"For what reason? What was her motive for shooting Manon Vinet? What it was, of course, was the baby; but police had no knowledge of that. She feared that Manon would expose Gerald Summerston, and Flora couldn't have that any more than could her aunt."

"And you think," said Jury, "she also shot Moira Quinn?"

"Yes. She probably knew that Summerston was Moira Quinn's lover, too."

"But he was a sick man in his seventies," said Melrose.

Tom's laugh was a short bark. "How sick do you have to be and since when has age ever stopped a man as sexually obsessed as Gerald Summerston? How many women did Summerston seduce? By her own admission, Eleanor Summerston had to let a maid go because she showed too much interest in Gerald, and Betsy Quinn seconded that. And those were only two they knew about. How many over the years could there have been that Eleanor *didn't* know about? He was a man of unquenchable thirst and no more control over it than a raging alcoholic. A sex addict. No woman was out of bounds."

"Including Flora Flood?"

"Absolutely including Flora Flood. I think she was in love with Summerston and I think Eleanor suspected it and it put her in a hell of a bind. After all, she could fire the maids and the kitchen help; but she could hardly throw out her own niece. Also, she was probably never sure about Flora."

"Manon's baby was in line for a fortune," said Jury. "According to Gabrielle Belrose, 'she had it in writing.' Manon, who was nobody's fool, got Gerald Summerston to sign something about the baby's being his; otherwise she'd have gone to his wife and laid the whole thing out. All he had to do was sign over a small fortune to this child which would be arranged as a pay off after his wife died. Something like that. Otherwise, she wouldn't have allowed him to leave her in Paris, himself unfettered and with no obligation. And that's a document Gabrielle has in her possession."

"But any decent legal team could blow that out of the water," said Melrose.

"I'm sure, but would Gerald have wanted Eleanor around to watch its being blown?"

"So that would show that Zillah is his daughter, but what about all the rest of this: there's no evidence, Tom. How do we prove that Flora shot all these people? Where's the evidence?"

"We'll go and get some." Tom rose. "Tomorrow morning. Too late tonight, so let's have another." He raised his pint. "Cheers."

39

"Where are we going?" said Melrose the next morning as they left the Old Success.

"Watermeadows," said Tom.

"That'll take six hours to drive." They were bundling themselves into Melrose's car.

"We go to Exeter airport then to London City. M1 to Northampton takes less than two hours. That is, if you don't mind leaving this car at the airport."

Melrose started the Rolls. "I've got others."

It took about an hour to get to London City Airport from Exeter.

Once they got their hired car onto the M1, Jury said, "How do we know she's alone?"

"We don't, but I'd bet she is. She doesn't go out much," said Melrose. "However—mobile, somebody?" When Jury pulled out his, Melrose said, "Call Ardry End."

Ruthven answered and Jury said, "Lord Ardry wants a word, Ruthven."

Melrose said into the mobile, "Is Gerrard there? I want to talk to him."

It sounded as if there was a bit of a scuffle in this transfer of news, but Melrose assumed there was always a scuffle by way of getting Gerrard. "There's something I want you to do. Go to Watermeadows . . . what? Oh, just make up some excuse. I simply want you to get Bub out of the way . . . no, nothing's going to explode. Keep Bub out of the library for a couple of hours; keep him out for as long as we're there . . . no, we're not there yet, but we will be in less than an hour and we want to talk to Flora Flood alone. Right." Melrose was about to hang up into the chatter on the other end and then said, "But if anyone comes in before we get there, call me back on Mr. Jury's number." He passed the mobile back to Jury, who gave Gerrard the number and added. "We should be there in another forty, fifty minutes. Okay."

Tom took the phone, said, "Listen Gerrard, when you get there find out where Flora Flood is and if anyone else is on the premises. Call back."

In another twenty minutes, Jury's mobile tweeted. He answered, listened. "Okay, thanks." He turned to the others. "Flora's in the kitchen. Cook's gone to the Waitrose in Northampton. There's nobody else around. Gerrard's got Bub up in his room playing some game." He said to Gerrard, "Just keep him out of the library, which is where we intend to be."

Tom took out his own mobile and put in a call to Brierly, who wasn't there. "Get him to call me, Brownell. It's important."

Twenty minutes later they were pulling up in front of Watermeadows. In another minute, the door was opened by Flora Flood herself. Seeing the three of them, she looked startled, then made a try at looking pleased, and failing at that, settled for composure. "Come in, though I can't imagine—"

"You can't?" said Tom. Then to Jury, "Hold on. It's Brierly." He smiled at Flora. "I wonder, could we go into the library?" He turned away for a moment to speak to Brierly. "Watermeadows? No, now. Really. Bye."

Looking even more uncertain, she ushered them into the library, which was colder than the foyer, its fire as yet unlit.

"What's this all about? What's it to do with Inspector Brierly?"

"We're just waiting for him."

"Again, why? What's this *about*?"

"We needed to have another look at the scene. You know, the crime scene."

"Why? Has something else happened?"

Tom gave a short laugh. "I'd say quite a lot has happened since the night your husband was shot."

"It's cold in here. I'm going to light the fire." She started to kneel by the grate, but Jury pulled her up. "We can do that."

"I'm perfectly capable—"

"I know you are."

"Do you mind if I get the whisky? Or do you want to do that too?"

"No, go ahead. Just don't open any drawers." Jury smiled, watched her as he got the fire going in the grate.

At the drinks table, she pulled over heavy tumblers, picked up the bottle of Glenlivet and turned, saying, "This suit you?"

"Admirably," said Melrose.

She pulled the stopper from the bottle, and when Flora turned again, she had a gun in her hand.

"I don't know what game this is, but I'm not playing. When Inspector Brierly's car pulls up, we'll all of us walk to the door, only one of us will have a gun in his back. You," she said to Melrose. She crooked her finger. "Come on."

Melrose heard a familiar clicking, not the safety on the gun, something else. When he heard it again, he started walking toward her. "Why don't you put that down, Flora. You're only making things worse for yourself."

"For *myself.* That's very funny."

"You've already shot three people. We know about Manon Vinet and Moira Quinn." Melrose took two more steps forward.

Jury called, "Melrose! Don't—!"

The shot that didn't hit him came just as the chandelier swung. The second shot went wild as Gerrard dropped to the floor, just a few feet from Flora, but the short distance was made up when he flew at her. They both fell, and Jury was on the gun as Tom went down on one knee.

"Tom!" yelled Jury.

"Nothing, nothing." He took a bloody handkerchief from his leg. "Told you we'd get the evidence."

"My God, Gerrard," said Melrose. "I thought you could manage the chandelier; I didn't expect you to come with it!"

"Yeah? So maybe I can get me a place with the Met?" Gerrard sported a huge grin.

"Or Cirque du Soleil," said Melrose.

PART VII
Sundowner

40

"*B*ugsy Malone? Who the bloody hell'd you get to ride this horse? Danny DeVito? Bloody hell, George! *Bugsy*?" Gerrard stared up at the pale blue sky.

"His first name is Burgess. Now, if you were a jockey, would you want to go by 'Burgess'?"

"It ain't any worse than 'Gerrard,'" said Gerrard, chewing his gum fast. "He ain't no Lester Piggott."

"And this horse ain't no Nijinsky," said George.

Aggrieved wasn't sure he liked *that* remark.

"Sorry," said George.

"Oh, that's—"

"I wasn't apologizing to you." George smiled.

This argument between Gerrard and George Jenks had ensued weeks before during a fruitless exchange between Gerrard and Sydney over which of them should ride Aggrieved in the Sundown Stakes in March at the Sundowner Racecourse, a little one-mile, three-furlong track not far from Northampton.

George had sensibly pointed out that neither one of them was a licensed jockey, and no, there wasn't time enough to get a license in the short while before the race. In any event, the racing authority was unlikely to grant Gerrard the right to ride the horse. Even if he could *prove* he was sixteen (through whatever shady North London connections he might have), since sixteen wasn't *eighteen* and that's how old he'd have to be to get a license.

"Bloody hell!" was Gerrard's response to everything, including Danny DeVito's next film about corruption at the race track, called *Black Track* (a film made up by Gerrard, in which Danny would not be appearing).

Sydney, even after all of her arguing, sympathized, saying it was pretty damned sad that after the heroism Gerrard had shown the night of Flora Flood's "shooting up Watermeadows," Gerrard was not to be rewarded.

George agreed. "But I'm not the BHA; I don't set the rules. Sorry. You'd make a very good jockey, Gerrard. You should go to racing school."

The word *school* didn't meet with much approval. But then George went on:

"You're old enough right now to do morning workouts if you can get someone to take you on."

That compliment had Gerrard chewing his gum a lot faster. "How'd I do that, then?"

"Oh, I could probably help. But you'd still best go to racing school."

Help was met with enough enthusiasm to mitigate the second mention of *school*. It also restored Gerrard's faith in a trainer who would take on someone named "Bugsy." Gerrard even managed a bit of gratitude. "Well, thanks, George. You think you could get me a job? I know you got a lot of clout."

George Jenks smiled. "Some. So are we okay, then, about Aggrieved and the Sundown Stakes? In another week or ten days we maybe can go to Cheltenham. Prize money there's a couple of million."

Gerrard was chewing his gum so fast now he was close to breaking a molar. "Bloody hell!"

"Don't think we can get into that at this late date, though. Sorry I brought it up." No, he wasn't. "So we'll stick with the Sundown Stakes. Even there, the money's not bad. Two hundred thousand."

A race which was to be run on this new sunny day in early March. It was nearly three months since Flora Flood had been arrested for the triple murder of Tony Servino, Manon Vinet and Moira Quinn. Arrested, indicted and arraigned, she had pled innocent.

Her defense continued to be that her husband had come to Watermeadows to talk her out of the divorce. "You were the only one who heard what Tony Servino had to say, so you could use that to your own advantage." Finally, she had admitted that his reason for coming had had nothing to do with the divorce—something he himself had initiated—but to do with Gerald Summerston's demands that Tony silence Ernest Temple.

But she couldn't make that stick against the further charge of attempted murder, since there'd been witnesses to her shooting of Tom Brownell, even though she'd meant to shoot Melrose Plant. "Oh, well," Melrose had said, "we all make mistakes."

It would be some months before Flora's trial. But since even Pete Apted (along with every other defense attorney) had turned the case down, the outcome was certain. Apted had said, "My God, she kills three people to save the reputation of one dead guy? Even Churchill, who never quit, would have yelled 'Quit!' to that."

So on this blue day in March, with the horse in his trailer, they had set off for the Sundowner Racecourse.

Aggrieved, who hadn't run a race in years, and had been trained for only three months—but trained by George Jenks, so it might as well have been three years—went calmly into the stable, where Sydney, who was acting as groom, began wiping him down. And brushing him. Aggrieved, whose coat managed to shine even in the shadows, needed no brushing. Aggrieved, with his never-lost racing demeanor and looking like the epitome of a thoroughbred racehorse, waited patiently for this unnecessary process to finish, since it was Sydney who was doing it. Because Sydney was his Person. Not simply his favorite person, but his *Person*. She should have been his jockey, for with Sydney on his back, he could have won not just this small-stakes race, but the Royal Ascot, the King George, the Derby, the Gold Cup, the St. Leger, every race run. "You can't win 'em all" did not apply where Aggrieved and Sydney were concerned. But, worse luck, he was to be ridden by some bugger named "Bugsy." Oh, well.

"I just lost me hundred-quid bet!" cried Mrs. Withersby. The Jack and Hammer was closed; everybody was at the track, all of the regulars —Melrose, Diane, Joanna, Trueblood—and the staff (not very big): Dick Scroggs and his char.

"Damned race is a walkout!" she added.

"Walk*over*, Withers. But congratulations on getting one syllable right," said Trueblood.

They were all gathered, leaning on the rail, waiting for Aggrieved to come pounding alone out of the gate. "And you didn't lose, for God's sakes; you just didn't win," said Trueblood.

"Not winning's losing," she yelled at him. "Always has been, always will be." She turned on George Jenks. "You cheat, you swindler, you rip-off artist!"

George was undisturbed. "Mrs. Withersby, it's the rules of the race. Nothing I can do if all the other horses pull out. The race is voided. There's no betting."

"Oh, *yeah*? You're prob'ly why they did. You could've poisoned their food, hammered on their hooves—"

"Come on, Withers," said Trueblood. "You're being ridiculous."

But George went on: "Tell you what. If Aggrieved wins, if you place your bet with me, I'll double it."

"What? Give you me hundred quid that's two months' rent? You think I'm crazy?"

"Yes," said Trueblood.

"Ya flamin' fairy, shut up!"

Jury, also standing at the fence, was amazed at what George then said.

"Okay, then." He pulled his wallet from his back pocket. "Suppose I give you your winnings *now*, as long as you promise if Aggrieved loses, you'll give me back *my* hundred?"

Even Withersby had to take a step back at this offer. Even *she* was convinced this guy must be honest. "Oh, bloody hell, never mind."

George repocketed his money and turned to Diane.

Diane had her binoculars trained on the starting gate. She loved the binoculars, which were black, strong and so small she considered wearing them in place of her pearls. They could pick out anything, including a couple way up there at the top who were pawing one another to perdition.

To her, George said, "That must have cost you, sweetheart. Only two horses pulled out for sickness and leg trouble. That left six. Six horses' entry fees."

She turned her binoculars to look at his face. "Oh, it wasn't all that much. Entry fee was only fifteen thousand pounds per. I just wanted to make certain Aggrieved won."

"Hell, that's ninety thousand."

"How wonderful, Georgie, you can do arithmetic."

George Jenks, thought Jury, was so good-humored, good-natured and equable, he was amazed that Diane Demorney could have rattled him into leaving.

But maybe it hadn't been a rattle at all. Maybe the two of them were so much alike that they were at a loss.

Jury thought of Tony Servino and Daisy Brownell and was sad. He wished to God they were here, that they hadn't lost. He wished they'd won.

Aggrieved had come out of the gate now and was running along the middle of the track, Bugsy Malone way up in the saddle, looking as if he were competing with a dozen other jockeys.

George said, "Even without the buy-off, we could have won, sweetheart."

Binoculars down, Diane turned to him. "That's exactly what you said, Georgie, before you walked out the door: 'We could have won, sweetheart.'"

"I did?" He gave her a long look, put his hands on her shoulders and pulled her in as Aggrieved rounded the bend and thundered by. The kiss was not just a touch on the cheek but a hard one on the lips.

Rudeness was the only thing running with the horse. No contest here, no being pushed to the rail. Instead, cameras were pulled from pockets and purses. Click. Click. Click. Click.

Except for Richard Jury's, not because he was more polite but because his phone, as usual, was powerless.

How wonderful! he thought. Here we poor sods go through our lives being crammed and crowded, passed up and galloped by, pushed and prodded, whipped and pounded on, but then there's that kiss. A kiss that's always there, and if not right here, then in some otherwhere, galloping alone in the middle of the track, pounding down the earth, running uncontested, churning up the surface, flying for the finish—

That kiss was a walkover.

And wonderfully, Aggrieved won.